CONSENT

CONSENT

NANCY OHLIN

SIMON PULSE

New York   London   Toronto   Sydney   New Delhi

This book is a work of fiction. Any references to historical events, real people, or real places are used fictitiously. Other names, characters, places, and events are products of the author's imagination, and any resemblance to actual events or places or persons, living or dead, is entirely coincidental.

SIMON PULSE

An imprint of Simon & Schuster Children's Publishing Division

1230 Avenue of the Americas, New York, New York 10020

First Simon Pulse hardcover edition November 2015

Text copyright © 2015 by Nancy Ohlin

Jacket magnetic words photograph copyright © 2015 by Thinkstock/TimHesterPhotography

Jacket blackboard photograph copyright © 2015 by Thinkstock/Maridav

For information about special discounts for bulk purchases, please contact

Simon & Schuster Special Sales at 1-866-506-1949 or business@simonandschuster.com.

The Simon & Schuster Speakers Bureau can bring authors to your live event.

For more information or to book an event, contact the Simon & Schuster Speakers Bureau

at 1-866-248-3049 or visit our website at www.simonspeakers.com.

Book designed by Karina Granda

The text of this book was set in Adobe Caslon Pro.

Manufactured in the United States of America

2 4 6 8 10 9 7 5 3 1

Library of Congress Cataloging-in-Publication Data

Ohlin, Nancy.

Consent / by Nancy Ohlin. —First Simon Pulse hardcover edition.

pages cm

Summary: "An intense bond between high school senior Bea and her music teacher turns into a passionate affair, but when their affair turns into a scandal, Bea wonders if their romance was ever real."—Provided by publisher.

ISBN 978-1-4424-6490-2 (hc)

[1. Teacher-student relationships—Fiction. 2. Love—Fiction. 3. Musicians—Fiction. 4. High schools—Fiction. 5. Schools—Fiction.] I. Title.

PZ7.O41404Co 2015

[Fic]—dc23

2015014970

ISBN 978-1-4424-6492-6 (eBook)

For Christopher

CONSENT

PROLOGUE

The police officer switches on the video camera, and its red light blink blink blinks at me.

"Are you comfortable? Do you want a different chair?" he asks.

"No, thanks, I'm good."

His smile as he regards me is kind and fatherly; his eyes, not so much. On the table between us are an unwrapped granola bar and two cups of shiny Styrofoam water.

"Don't be nervous. It's just us," he says.

He flips open a notebook and scribbles something in police hieroglyphics. And then the questions start.

I tell my story to the blinking red light. As I do, I try to remember:

Maintain eye contact.

Keep it simple.

Stay as close to the truth as possible.

ONE

It's the first day of senior year—or as Plum puts it, "The Year Before Our Real Lives Can Finally Begin." At lunch she and I eat Kraft cheese and French dressing sandwiches together in the cafetorium.

What an awful word: "cafetorium." It sounds like a monster in a Syfy movie. The reality isn't much better. At Andrew Jackson High School, a.k.a. A-Jax, it is a vast, impersonal, mental-asylum space with milk-colored walls and the forever stench of boiled meat. The inmates within are many, noisy, and dangerous.

Plum and I started Mad Sandwich Mondays sophomore year—the "wise fool" year, the year when we thought we would be stuck in the never-ending loop of high school and not–high school for eternity. We take turns bringing each other odd combinations, like peanut butter–cucumber, pineapple-mayo, and bacon–Marshmallow Fluff.

"This is actually good," I say, taking a bite of my sandwich. "It's weirdly comforting."

"My mom used to eat these when she was little. Hey, Bea?"

"What?"

"Have you thought about what I said? About Harvard? Because the Early Action deadline is November first, and we should really get cracking on the application."

"Oh, yeah. That."

Over the summer Plum got the idea that we should go to Harvard together. She thinks we have a good chance of getting in because we have the two highest GPAs in school. I told her that my cousin Jin didn't get into Harvard, and he had a 4.0, perfect regular *and* subject SATs, and a letter of recommendation from a U.S. senator, from some swank internship. Of course, this didn't faze her one bit. The word "impossible" is not in Plum's vocabulary.

Now she reaches into her backpack and extracts her sparkly gold notebook—nicknamed "The Golden Notebook," after Doris Lessing's novel. On the first page are an A list and a B list of the colleges she wants us to apply to. *Harvard* is at the very top and has a big pink heart around it. Included, too, are a bunch of due dates and requirements: transcripts, test scores, the Common App, et cetera. The guidance counselor,

Miss Beaven, is supposed to be doing all this, but with 798 seniors to get through, she's probably slammed.

Plus, she's Miss Beaven. Plum and I try not to talk to her or any other adults at A-Jax unless it's absolutely necessary.

Plum sits up with an excited flutter of hands. "I know! Let's go on a road trip to Boston. Columbus Day weekend! I've heard it really helps to visit the schools, do the tours, and suck up to the admissions people." She blushes. "I mean, 'make a good impression on.'"

I laugh. "It's okay to say 'suck up.' Just not to their faces."

Her eyes light up. "So we can go?"

"No, that's not what I—"

But she is already looking at her calendar, rattling off dates, and talking about borrowing her parents' Prius so we can save on gas.

I eat my Kraft cheese and French dressing sandwich and let Plum's Disney-cheerful voice wash over me.

Maybe I should remind her that the heroine of *The Golden Notebook* has a mental breakdown.

Maybe I should just skip college altogether and become a cafetorium lady.

No, I'm not one of those slackers who want to check out after high school and drift aimlessly through life. Not like my brother, Theo, who at age twenty-nine still works at CVS, shares a house with six other guys, and plays guitar for a garage band called the Angry Weasels. I think he thinks that beer is one of the four major food groups.

I'm also not depressed. I know all about depression from health class, the not eating and not sleeping and not wanting to get out of bed, and that's definitely not me.

It's just that I don't know what I'm supposed to do next. Pretty much the only thing I enjoy doing besides hanging out with Plum is playing the piano. But there's no way I can become a professional musician. Plus, lately, that part of my life has lost its spark and momentum—I'm not sure why.

Also, it's not like anyone in my family shows any interest in my future whatsoever. Sometimes I envy those kids with the pushy helicopter parents, like Cassie Lindstrom's mom, who videotapes her voice lessons and postmortems them afterward, or Zach Cormier's dad, who puts his dance clips on YouTube and tweets about them:

@zachcorm made it to the finals at Nationals! Woot!

The only person who's pushing me forward is Plum. And really, she's just imposing her own blueprint on me, because as far as she's concerned, we're identical twins.

But we're not. We are so not.

I love her, but she has no clue. About my future, my past, anything.

Although maybe that's something we have in common.

Woot.

Two

My afternoon is a blur of classes: AP bio, then AP English, then U.S. history. I'm already pretty knowledgeable in most of these subjects, on top of which Plum isn't in any of my sections, so I have no one to make faces at the teachers with. I picture nine long months of doodling and playing hangman by myself. I wish I could cut and show up only for the quizzes and tests, but apparently, there are rules about that sort of thing.

My last class of the day is music history. I needed an arts elective, and it was either that or photography with Mrs. Lutz, whose nickname is "Lutz the Klutz" for no other reason than it rhymes. Plum calls this the "random cruelty of youth." I call it stupid. In any case, I picked music history, even though I probably won't learn anything new, considering. Besides, it's only for this semester, three days a week.

I find a seat in the back, near the window, so that I can doodle in peace. The classroom is big and bright, part of the recently renovated performing arts wing. We used to be a regular old high school before we got rebranded as a "Campus for Baccalaureate and Performing Arts." They built a bunch of new classrooms as well as a dance studio, black box theater, and keyboard lab. So, basically, A-Jax is a fancy-pants school now, even though most of it—the cafetorium, the halls, the randomly cruel student body—feels exactly the same.

The teacher stands at the blackboard with his back to the class. He must be new; I've never seen him before.

I crane my neck to get a glimpse of his face. No luck. From this angle, I can only make out broad shoulders and longish, curlyish brown hair.

He writes on the blackboard:

Mr. Rossi

Music History

1. *The Baroque Period*
2. *The Transition to Classical*
3. *The Classical Era*
4. *The Early Romantics*
5. *The Late Romantics*
6. *20th-Century Modernism*

The bell rings. Nelson Geiser hurries into the room and sits down across the aisle from me. As he leans toward me, I smell Axe body spray and potato chips. "This is our second class together," he says with a toothy grin. "By the way, did I mention that you're looking very comely today?"

I give him an eye roll. Nelson has been on-and-off hitting on me since last spring, when I made the mistake of agreeing to be his lab partner in AP chem. His M.O. is to "compliment" me with vocab-board words: "comely," "resplendent," "pulchritudinous." Scoring with Smart Girls 101. I suppose I should be flattered by his attention, but I'm totally not.

"What are you doing Saturday night, comely wench? Methinks we should go out," Nelson says with a leer.

"Methinks no," I reply.

"Splendid. I'll take that as a maybe?"

I guess "no" means something else in Nelson World.

Mr. Rossi turns from the blackboard and scans the class. Oh my *God*, he's cute. Chiseled features and sexy stubble . . . Are teachers allowed to be that good-looking?

"Good afternoon, everyone. I'm Mr. Rossi, and this is

eighth-period music history," he says. He has a nice voice, deep and British.

There are a couple of appreciative catcalls from across the room. Wendy Stiles and Mallory Meecham, the senior sluts—no surprise there. Mr. Rossi blushes and coughs and clears his throat. He pulls some index cards out of his pocket, reads over them quickly, and launches into the first-day-of-class drill: roll call, rules and regs, a detailed explanation of the grading system, and the handing out of the syllabus. Poor guy—I guess he's not used to the wonderful world of raging hormones and low IQs.

"Music history. Can anyone tell me what that means?" he asks.

"The, um, history of music?" says someone in the front row.

"Yes, but is it the history of *all* music? Why don't we parse that phrase, 'music history'?"

Now, *there's* a vocab-board word: "parse." Although coming from him, it seems quaint and nineteenth-century versus obnoxious and Nelson-esque.

"What is music? It is a combination of sounds intended to produce harmony, form, beauty, and emotional expression. As far as we know, music has been on this earth for over fifty thousand years, dating back to our earliest ancestors," he continues.

Nelson scratches his armpits like a chimpanzee and winks at me. Really attractive. In front of him Aziza Sayid texts under her desk without looking. I have yet to master that skill, and the one time I tried, I ended up sending a message to Plum that auto-corrected into: *Meet my laundry.* Sometimes she says that to make me laugh: "Bea, meet my laundry!"

If I knew how to stealth-text, I would consider sending a message to Plum: *Have you seen the new music history teacher? When did A-Jax lift its policy of hiring only appearance-challenged old people?*

"In this course we will not be studying the history of music from the time of the cavemen. Our starting point will be the sixteen hundreds"—Mr. Rossi taps his chalk against the words *The Baroque Period*—"and our ending point will be the twenty-first century and beyond," he says, now tapping *The Future of Music.* "Furthermore, we will not be studying the music of all cultures. Our focus will be Western music, primarily Western classical music. That's 'classical' with a little *c.* By the way, can anyone tell me the difference between 'classical' with a little *c* and 'Classical' with a capital *C*?"

Silence.

"Anyone?"

More silence.

I raise my hand.

"Yes? You in the back," Mr. Rossi says, apparently to distinguish me from the dozens of others with their hands up.

I sit up in my chair and smile. He smiles back. *That smile.* For a moment I forget what I was going to say.

"Did you have something you wanted to . . . ?" he prompts me.

"Yes. Hi! So, 'Classical' with a capital *C* describes a period in Western musical history between the middle of the eighteenth century and the early nineteenth century. 'Classical' with a little *c* describes a style of music that follows certain forms and conventions that were popular during that period. Like Mozart's or Haydn's music—or certain works by Stravinsky or Poulenc, who were twentieth-century composers. Also, people often use the term 'classical music' to describe any music that's not pop, rock, jazz, folk, world music, et cetera."

Mr. Rossi blinks at me. "Yes, that's very . . . um, that's excellent. Thank you."

"You are so brilliant. It is such a turn-on," Nelson whispers.

I give him a withering look. He's being disgusting; plus, he's ruining my special moment with Mr. Rossi.

"Like I said, we will be focusing primarily on Western classical music," Mr. Rossi goes on. "By 'Western,' we're talking about North America and Europe—and, of course, Russia, which geographically and culturally straddles both Europe and Asia."

Some students giggle at the word "straddles." Mr. Rossi blushes again as he turns back to the blackboard. Has he never taught high school before? He's going to have to develop a thicker skin. Still, it's very quaint and nineteenth-century of him—the blushing. It's also a paradox, because he seriously looks like a twenty-first-century sex god.

He glances at another index card and writes *1600–1750* next to *The Baroque Period*.

"Let's begin with the baroque period, shall we?" he says over his shoulder. "This is an era we associate with such composers as Bach, Handel, Vivaldi, Telemann, Scarlatti, Rameau, and Couperin. The word 'baroque' comes from the Italian word *barocco,* meaning 'imperfect pearl.' Why is baroque music like an imperfect pearl?"

Ornamentation, I think. But I don't want to be that annoying serial-hand-raising girl, so I keep it to myself. I lean over my notebook and doodle an oyster shell with a big, shiny pearl inside. My hair falls across my face, which gives me a useful cover for shameless ogling.

"Pearls are supposed to be smooth," Mr. Rossi says. "But baroque music is anything but smooth because of ornamentation. Here, let me show you what I mean."

He strides over to a piano in the corner and pulls the heavy brown quilted cover off of it. I crane my neck to see. *Whoa,* it's a brand-new Steinway. A full seven-foot grand, all gleaming and black like polished obsidian.

Mr. Rossi sits down and curls his fingers over the keyboard. He begins the aria from Bach's Goldberg Variations. I generally don't like Bach, but I love the Goldberg Variations. I especially love the aria, which is a seamless mash-up of happy, sad, and religious experience.

On top of which, Mr. Rossi is an amazing pianist. He plays Bach like Glenn Gould, like he's pouring his entire soul into each note. Where did he learn to do that? Listening to him, I feel as though I'm in a concert hall in New York City or London or Paris.

"Do you hear this little musical embellishment?" He stops in the middle of a measure and executes a lightning-quick trill. His voice has grown more animated; he seems to be in his element, sitting at the piano. "This is an example of an ornament. Ornaments are like decorations, in that they are not necessary to carry along the melody line of the piece. I'll play the same measure *without* the ornament, and you'll be able to hear the difference."

He starts playing again—first just that measure, then the whole piece from the beginning, without ornaments. Aziza continues texting. Nelson continues being Nelson.

I tune them out and play along on my knees, quietly humming the aria under my breath. I follow Mr. Rossi's perfect profile as he closes his eyes and leans into the music.

I think I'm going to enjoy this class after all.

THREE

After school Plum and I walk over to her house, which is what we've been doing almost every day since we met in ninth grade. It's way better than my house for about a billion reasons. She and her family live on Lark Street in a sprawling green Victorian. They moved from Philadelphia to Eden Grove three years ago because they wanted a yard and a dog and a "slower pace," whatever that is. Eden Grove is full of people like them: rich transplants from big cities who crave U-pick farms, used bookstores, and expensive restaurants pretending to be not-expensive restaurants.

Mostly, I think Eden Grove is pretentious and boring.

As Plum and I walk, we discuss teachers. "Who did you get for your afternoon classes?" I ask.

"Mr. Rodriguez for chem, Mrs. Erlich for French, Ms. Lee for calculus, and Mr. Ferguson for English," Plum replies. "What about you?"

"Mr. Sappenfield for bio, Mr. Smith for English, Ms. Hillier for U.S. History, and Mr. Rossi for music history." I pause. "Do you know him? Mr. Rossi?"

"I think I saw him in my study hall. Is he the one who looks like Kit Harington?"

"Hmm. Yeah, I could see that."

Plum giggles. "Bea! Do you have a crush?"

"Right. Very funny."

"Because you haven't dated anyone since that violin guy."

"Seriously, Plum. *Cello.* You really are illiterate about music. And I'm not going to date a teacher, that's gross."

"If I were going to date a teacher, it would be Mr. Anderson in *The Perks of Being a Wallflower.* Or Mr. Thackeray in *To Sir, With Love.*"

"If we're dating imaginary people, I would probably go with Batman."

"You would!"

"I wonder if he has sex hanging upside down?"

We laugh and hurry our steps.

At Plum's house we hopscotch to the door along the path of inlaid stone: slate, then jasper, then quartz, then repeat. This is another one of our traditions, along with Mad Sandwich Mondays. On either side of the path is her mom's garden, which is a profusion of zinnias, sunflowers, herbs, and vegetables. The late-afternoon sun makes everything look warm, sleepy, and hazy-golden.

Plum pauses mid-hop, plucks a cherry tomato, and plops it into her mouth. "Someone's home. The Volvo's here. I wonder what's for dinner?"

"Isn't today spicy chicken stew day?"

"Oh, right! *Doro wat.* You know my family's recipe rotation better than I do."

"Tuesdays are Swedish food, Wednesdays are make your own tacos, Thursdays are pasta or pizza, Fridays are sushi from Tokyo Palace, and Saturdays and Sundays are anything goes," I rattle off.

"I am *so* impressed!"

"Yeah, well, I'm very impressive."

Once inside Plum drops her backpack on the shiny oak floor. I set mine down carefully on the front hall table next to a ceramic bowl full of keys. Shakespeare, who is part Saint Bernard, part German shepherd, and part lots of other things, lopes out of the living room. He greets us with a friendly bark and slobbery kisses.

"Mom? Dad? We're *hoooome!*" Plum shouts.

"Pernilla!"

Mrs. Sorenson emerges from the kitchen holding a glass of white wine in one hand and a spatula in the other. Her red sundress is striking against her dark brown skin, and her long black hair spills down her back. She looks like a model, which is what she was before she became a full-time mom and author. She writes picture books about a frog named Sir Ribbit and is practically a rock star in the under-six set.

She kisses Plum's forehead and then mine. Her scent is a mix of Chanel No. 5 and sautéed onions. "Hello, my loves. How was your first day back?"

"Great!" says Plum.

"So boring," I say at the same time.

Mrs. Sorenson touches my cheek. "It's senioritis, darling. I had it too. Honestly, I couldn't get to college fast enough."

"Where's Daddy?" Plum asks.

"He's on his way home. His flight from L.A. just landed. Bea, sweetheart, you're welcome to stay for dinner."

"Thank you, Mrs. Sorenson."

"You girls can help me with the salad. I found the loveliest spinach at the farmer's market this afternoon. And it's organic!"

Mrs. Sorenson turns and heads back to the kitchen, still raving about the spinach. Plum, Shakespeare, and I trail after her. As we pass the dining room, I notice that the table has already been set for four. Everything looks so festive: the crystal vase flush with half-open roses, the pearly-white wedding china edged with gold, the silver candlestick holders. Mrs. Sorenson always says that nice things aren't meant to gather dust and that every day is a special occasion.

She is pretty much a grown-up version of Plum.

In the white, sun-dappled kitchen, the *doro wat* bubbles on the stove. An array of ingredients covers the marble counters: garlic, ginger, half an onion, a stick of butter, and a carton of eggs. Jazz piano plays from an iPod dock—Oscar Peterson or maybe Bill Evans. The finches, Hansel and Gretel, twitter at each other in their ornate antique cage.

On the refrigerator is a photo magnet of Plum from when she was in kindergarten. With her curly Renoir hair, enormous blue eyes, and caramel complexion, she looks almost the same as she does now. Next to the magnet is a crayon drawing of three dinosaurs and the words "I LOV YOU MOMY DADY ROARRRRR."

Plum tears a piece of *injera* and offers me half. "Can Bea and I go to Boston Columbus Day weekend?" she asks her mom through a mouthful of bread. "We want to visit Harvard really badly. We're going to apply Early Action!"

"Wait, what?" I whisper to Plum. She waves her hand to shush me.

"Not Princeton?" Mrs. Sorenson says, sounding disappointed. She and Mr. Sorenson both went there.

"We *do* want to apply to Princeton, Mommy. Just not Early

Action. So is it okay if we go to Boston? And can we borrow the Prius? And can I ask Aunt Jessika and Ingrid if we can stay with them for the weekend? Please, please, please?"

Mrs. Sorenson laughs. "You have it all figured out, don't you? Well, it sounds like a fine plan. Let me talk to your father first."

Plum flashes me a triumphant smile. "*Yes!* Road trip!"

I frown at her: *But I haven't agreed to this yet.*

She gives me a breezy look back: *Just trust me!*

"You girls might want to fit in some other school visits while you're there," Mrs. Sorenson says as she dips a wooden spoon into a tin labeled ETHIOPIAN BERBERE. "Like maybe Tufts and BU and Wellesley? There are so many other good colleges, too."

"I'll have to ask my dad," I say, hedging. "I'll have to clear it with Mrs. Lugansky, too. She doesn't like it when I miss a lesson, and my lessons are always on Saturdays, and it's really hard to reschedule with her."

"I'm sure Scary Russian Lady will let you go," says Plum. "After all, this is about *college.*"

Her face is so shiny and hopeful, like she's talking about Christmas morning.

It's very hard to say no to Plum.

This is where I should tell her the truth. That I have no interest in Harvard or Princeton or any other college. That my dad wouldn't even notice if I went away for a weekend, any weekend. That Mrs. Lugansky is not a real person.

But it's been so long since I've lived in the world of facts that I'm not sure how to even start that conversation.

"I'll see what I can do," I promise without looking at her.

"Yay!" Plum grabs me in a fierce embrace that falls somewhere between bear hug and death grip.

The Sorensons are an effusive people.

Aside from the lying thing, Plum and I have a great friendship. We care about each other and watch each other's backs. Also, it's really easy to be with her; she's like a sister who is so familiar, like every-molecule-in-our-bodies familiar, that we can slip in and out of osmosis without the slightest effort.

I also love her parents and desperately wish I were a Sorenson.

When Plum and I first met, it was ninth grade, and she was the new girl who sat in front of me in English and raised her hand even more than I did. One day, during a discussion of *Romeo and Juliet,* she turned around and whispered: "Do you want to come over after school and meet my new dog? His name is Shakespeare, too." For some reason, I found this funny and burst out laughing. She laughed too. Mrs. Jacobs gave us a stern look before resuming a tedious speech about the individual versus society.

I accepted Plum's invitation. This wasn't like me at all,

since I generally kept to myself; even back then, I was way more "individual" than "society." I had some friends but no one really close. There was something so irresistibly sunny and smart about Plum, though.

So we went to her house. I met Shakespeare and also her perfect parents, including her dad, who is a famous architect. We played backgammon and Clue and Ping-Pong in her groovy retro basement. We watched silly YouTube videos on her laptop.

Soon I was over there all the time. At first Mrs. Sorenson seemed worried and asked me if my parents didn't miss me. When I told her that it was just my dad and that he worked late most nights, she got teary-eyed and made me a huge mug of hot chocolate with tiny marshmallows.

So later that fall, when Tommy Vacco called Plum "Fatso" in phys ed, I punched him. I actually punched him. It was my one and only time getting a detention. But it was worth it, and Tommy totally left her alone after that.

I try to imagine what it would be like if Plum went away to Harvard or wherever and I stayed in Eden Grove. Aside from missing her, I really can't spend the rest of my life here. If I do, I will turn into Theo. Or worse, my dad.

Maybe I should just follow Plum's lead on this college business. Adulthood by osmosis. I'm sure there are worse ways to grow up.

Four

Later that night I decide to practice piano for a bit before going to bed. It's been a while, but something about hearing Mr. Rossi has motivated me; I could have listened to him forever.

I'm so glad I didn't sign up for photography with Mrs. Lutz.

Dad is still at his office, preparing for a new trial. He's been texting me for the last couple of hours, giving a later ETA each time. *Feel free to order in Chinese* was the most recent one.

I'm tempted to text back: *I'm sorry, do I know you?* or *The owner of this phone has been kidnapped by demented squirrel-bots.* But I don't. Dad does not have a sense of humor.

I put the phone away and play some arpeggios to warm up. The piano is a Kawai upright with a scratchy walnut finish. It hasn't been tuned in all the years we've lived in this house, and it's missing the high F key.

Still, it's a piano.

Gradually, my random broken chords begin to fall into order: first a C-major arpeggio, then a D, then an E. I complete all the major arpeggios and move on to the minor ones. The sound swells and resonates in the two-story living room/dining room, which is enormous and sparsely furnished and therefore a bit echoey. Our development is named Pleasant Meadow, which is weird because there are no meadows in sight, pleasant or otherwise. The house used to belong to Dad's mom; she gave it to him after he moved back to Eden Grove and before she retired to Tucson, Arizona. Dad never bothered to buy more furniture beyond what Grandma Min left, though, including the old piano, which was Aunt Jeanine's, I guess, when she was a kid.

Cream Puff appears out of nowhere and leaps onto the bench. She head-butts my arm with a violent burst of affection and derails my A-minor arpeggio.

I continue playing with my left hand and scratch Cream Puff's ears with my right. She purrs and digs her knifelike claws into my lap. Until last week Cream Puff was just "Cat." She's a stray, and Dad doesn't want me taking in any more strays. The last one cost us five hundred dollars in vet bills and died anyway. The one before that turned out to be pregnant.

Dad said Cat would have to go back outside unless I found another owner for her. I tried really hard not to name her because I was afraid of getting attached. But I ran out of will-power, and besides, she's so darned beautiful: a fluffy marma-lade coat, an elegant lion nose, and amber eyes that will play nonstop stare-down with you. She's also homeless, so how can I turn her out? The nights are already starting to get chilly, and I've had zero success getting someone to adopt her. Not even Plum's family can take her because Mr. Sorenson is super allergic to cats.

After a while Cream Puff stops her furious digging and curls into a warm ball on my lap. I can feel her gravelly purrs through my thin cotton skirt.

My arpeggios gradually morph into Chopin's Etude Opus 25, Number 12, a.k.a. the "Ocean Etude." The word *étude* derives from the French word for "study"; many études help to hone a particular technique. The Ocean Etude is all about the technique of arpeggios.

But for me, it's all about the ocean. When I play it, I hear waves rising and breaking and crashing against the rocks. I've never actually been to the ocean, any ocean, but I figure it must be just like this.

See ocean would be at the top of *my* wish list, encircled in a big pink heart.

After Chopin, I go backward in time and start from the beginning. Bach's second Partita—I wonder if Mr. Rossi plays this one? Then Beethoven's Sonata Number 32, Opus 111, which has only two movements instead of the usual three and was one of the pieces he composed after becoming deaf.

Then I return to the nineteenth century with Schumann's Fantasy in C. Finally, I move on to the twentieth century with Rachmaninoff's "Little Red Riding Hood" étude and Ravel's "Jeux d'eau," meaning "water games."

It's almost eleven o'clock before I realize that I've been playing for three hours straight. I don't remember the last time I did that. I wonder if Mr. Rossi likes to practice late at night too? What kind of piano does he own? Where does he live? Does he live alone, or—

My phone buzzes, startling me. It's another text from Dad: *Home after midnight. See you in the morning.*

"Thanks, Dad," I say out loud.

It's probably just as well. I want to practice for a little bit longer, and it's always best to play when he isn't around.

FIVE

On Tuesday, I sleep through my phone alarm, and I can already tell that it's going to be one of those days. My blankets are in an agitated knot, and my muscles are tight with exhaustion. My head throbs with a sort-of migraine and the foggy vestiges of a dream.

I try to remember the dream. It was vague and sexy and disturbing. Was I in it? Who was I with? And then it comes to me: Mr. Rossi.

Why am I having X-rated dreams about him?

Obviously, *because,* I tell myself. Still, it's probably not a good idea to harbor sexual fantasies about one's teacher.

A sudden hacking noise makes me bolt straight up. On the floor next to my desk Cream Puff is throwing up on my backpack.

"That is not cool!" I yell at her. She regards me with a help-

less look, bucks, and proceeds to throw up some more.

Sighing, I slip on my glasses and get up to search for paper towels.

I pad down the hallway, which overlooks the great room with only a skeletal faux-wood guardrail separating me from the void. Rain spits against the skylights and makes a loud, steady, drumming sound.

Peering over the guardrail, I can see Dad's legal papers fanned across the dining room table, along with a coffee mug and an empty carton of Ben & Jerry's. He must have stayed up after he got home, to work. He gets like this whenever he has a trial.

Just before I reach the bathroom, I realize that the door to Theo's room is open. Curious, I poke my head inside.

Dad is on the floor, peering under the bed.

"Um . . . Dad?"

He turns and gives me a quick, embarrassed smile. He is wearing his fancy charcoal suit, a white shirt, and his lucky tie. The tie is maroon with invisible maroon stripes. His silvery-black hair—what there is of it—is still damp from the shower.

Plum once said Dad looks like an Asian George Clooney, but I don't buy it. I think he maybe *used* to be handsome, from my impression of his and Mom's wedding photo. But that photo is no more, so the details are a little fuzzy.

"I thought I heard a mouse in here. Hope I didn't wake you," he says.

"Dad, it's almost eight. I was supposed to be up, like, half an hour ago."

"Oh, right. Sorry, I'm a little . . ." His sentence trails off as he resumes his search for the mystery mouse.

I glance around Theo's room. It's basically unchanged since his last visit here, when he had to pick up some sweaters and also his old Yu-Gi-Oh! card collection for who knows what reason. Probably to sell it for beer money. Luckily, he left all his comic books behind. I don't care about his Green Lanterns and Fantastic Fours, but the Supermans and Batmans are absolutely not allowed to leave this house. He used to read them aloud to me when I was little, or at least he did on the few occasions when Dad forced him to babysit me.

Dad rises to his feet and brushes his hands against his pants legs. "I must have imagined it. How was your first day back? Do you need me to sign any forms?" He always asks me this, as though I were still in elementary school.

"No, no forms. The first day was fine."

"Did you get the classes you wanted?"

"Yes. Hey, Dad? Plum wants me to go to Boston with her on Columbus Day weekend, to visit some colleges."

Dad's phone buzzes in his jacket pocket. "Sounds good. Sorry, honey, I have to get this. I left you some lunch money by the coffeemaker. Feel free to use my credit card to make travel arrangements."

He pulls out his phone and turns his back to me. "Hello? Good morning, Carlos. Yeah, I was on Lexis all night, and I still haven't managed to dig up the right precedent on the 'defense of others' angle. . . ."

"Okay, then," I say to myself. Still, what did I expect? A sudden show of interest in my life?

I continue down the hallway and find a roll of paper towels in the bathroom. Hannah, our housekeeper, always keeps the cleaning supplies under the sink.

Back in my room Cream Puff is preening on my bed as though nothing happened. On top of my backpack a furry hair ball lies in a slimy pool of cat vomit. There are two other vomit piles on the floor. Luckily, they just missed my stack of prized vintage Nancy Drews.

"Thanks a lot," I say to Cream Puff. She blinks at me and continues licking her paw.

After I manage to restore my backpack to sort-of normal, I look around for something to wear. Fortunately, I find a pair of jeans and a green top on the closet floor that aren't wrinkly not that that should affect my wardrobe decisions in any way whatsoever.

Checking the time, I mentally calculate that I can brush my teeth, wash my face, put in my contacts, and scarf down a yogurt before I have to leave. If I catch a ride with Dad, I'll save ten minutes—plus, I won't have to walk in the rain.

I hear Dad's footsteps trotting down the stairs. More footsteps . . . then the front door opens and closes.

"Dad! Wait up!" I shout at the top of my lungs.

No answer.

For a moment I'm tempted to text him and tell him to come back. Something stops me, though—maybe the thought that he will say no? A girl can take only so much parental rejection in one lifetime.

But what am I going to do? I can't drive the other car, the ancient Subaru, because I haven't applied for a student parking permit yet. And I don't dare try to park without one since A-Jax is beyond draconian about rules and regs.

Sighing, I text Plum: *Can you guys give me a ride?*

She texts back immediately: *Yes, we'll be there @ 8:30! Do you want me to bring you a banana muffin? They're freshly baked!*

I really should just move in with the Sorensons.

Six

Plum has to meet with her chem lab group after school, so I need to kill some time. Later, we're planning to go to her house, take half of a practice SAT test, and reward ourselves with our favorite *Buffy* episode from season two—the one where Buffy and Angel finally, finally get together and enjoy about five minutes of happiness before all hell breaks loose in Hellmouth City.

Plum said that we should also watch a couple *Game of Thrones* episodes so we can stare at Kit Harington. Because that's just what I need, more reminders of how insanely handsome Mr. Rossi is.

I head over to the performing arts wing and try to find an empty practice room so I can work on the Schumann Fantasy. I don't have my sheet music with me, but I know most of it by heart. The hall swirls with students on their way to various extracurricular activities, including band practice, pointe class, and *West Side Story* tryouts. Bill Kist sings "Somewhere" to an invisible Maria. One of the Tisherman twins squeaks into his oboe. Siobhan Dunham does triceps stretches over her head as she ballet-walks with carefully turned-out feet.

Posters with sayings like EXCELLENCE IS NOT AN ACT BUT A HABIT and THERE IS NOT GREAT TALENT WITHOUT GREAT WILL-POWER cover the walls. I'm not sure why they make me feel cranky, but they do. "Excellence," "habit," "willpower" . . . they are totally made-up magazine words.

Rounding the corner, I peer into the practice rooms. Ugh, they're all filled; I should have gotten here sooner. Diondre Potts and his cute little freshman boyfriend are making out in one of them, so I could technically kick them out, but I don't have the heart.

I start to double back in the direction of the library when I notice that the light is on in the music history room.

Peeking through the glass pane, I see that no one is inside. The beautiful, brand-new Steinway is just sitting there, lonely and unused. I wiggle the door handle. It's unlocked.

I enter and close the door behind me. I make my way over to the piano and peel off the quilted cover.

My breath catches in my throat. The piano is even more glorious up close. The black lacquer finish is so shiny, it's practically liquid. There is a lovely thin red stripe that runs along the top of the keys.

A white handkerchief sits on top of the music rack. I pick it up, and the scent of eucalyptus and fresh soap wafts up. Could it be Mr. Rossi's? Quickly, I stuff it into my jeans pocket.

Then I sink onto the bench, settle my hands on the keyboard, and play a B-flat scale. The tone is like sweet crystal. I play a couple of low, loud chords. Their darkness is velvety and absolute.

For a moment I feel a frisson of guilt, like I'm cheating on my tired old piano back home.

I close my eyes, which forces me into that mental universe of touch and spatial instinct. Then I melt into the Schumann.

I love the Fantasy so, so much. I first heard it on the radio played by Alicia de Larrocha, who has small hands just like me but still managed to make the piece sound big and powerful. The first movement is lush and romantic, with the left hand accompaniment pulsing and rippling while the right hand navigates the melody.

Now comes the second movement, which is like Beethoven on steroids. My fingers leap and dive to manage the multiple octaves and dotted rhythm. I hum along with the dominant line while trying to bring out the different voices. There are so many things going on at once that I'm dizzy and heady with adrenaline.

My eyes snap open when I sense that someone is standing next to me.

Mr. Rossi.

"Oh!" I jump up from the bench and practically knock it down. "I'm sorry, I know I shouldn't be here. But I couldn't find a practice room, and the door was open, and—"

"You . . . play the piano," he says.

I stare at him.

"Yes, of course you play the piano. Sorry, I . . . Who is your teacher?"

"Mrs. Lugansky," I reply automatically. "My friend Plum calls her 'Scary Russian Lady.' "

His lips curl up in a hint of a smile. He has nice lips. And then I remember my dream from last night, and I have to force myself to think sad, serious thoughts—*dead puppies, starving orphans, global warming*—so he can't tell.

"She *used* to be my teacher," I add quickly. I really do have to stop propagating the Mrs. Lugansky lie. What if he asks me for her contact info so he can arrange piano lessons for his kids? Does he *have* kids? Is he married? He's not wearing a wedding ring.

"Used to be?" he prompts me.

"I'm, um, taking a break from lessons," I lie some more.

"I see."

He stands there, his expression inscrutable as he studies my face, then my hands, then the place on the keyboard where I left off. Am I in trouble? I'm not sure what I'm supposed to do, so I sit back down on the bench and reach for the quilted cover. I remember that I have his handkerchief in my pocket; will he notice that it's missing?

"You're incredible," he says finally. He looks away, flustered. "What I meant was, you're very gifted. But I suppose you've heard that many times."

Actually, no. "Thanks. Thank you. So, um . . . I guess you play the piano too?"

"Yes. I got my bachelor's degree in piano performance. Have you thought about mixing up the tempo more in the first movement?"

"Mix up the tempo? Why?"

"May I?"

Without waiting for my answer, Mr. Rossi sits down next to me and pushes the quilted cover aside. As he does, his tweed jacket grazes my bare arm. My skin tingles from the contact, and I want him to do that again: accidentally-on-purpose touch me. Although it was likely just an accident, and I really need to cut this out already.

He raises and lowers his elbows, then closes his eyes. He smells like his handkerchief, except warmer, sultrier. He launches into the first movement—initially at tempo, then more slowly, then with a series of fits and starts in the form of ritardandos and accelerandos. His interpretation is decidedly more measured and melancholy than mine, and more passionate, too.

He stops just before the shift to the second movement and turns to face me.

"So . . . what do you think?" he asks me.

Our legs are almost touching. Should I inch away? Or stay where I am?

"Beatrice?"

He knows my name. After just the one class. I should correct him and tell him that everyone calls me "Bea." But I love the way he says "Beatrice"—like a poem, and with that dreamy accent.

Oh, right, I need to respond. "Yes! Sorry! That was wonderful! Really deep and intense and tormented."

"Schumann was in a great deal of torment when he wrote this part."

"What was the matter with poor old Schumann?"

"Poor *young* Schumann. He was twenty-something at the time. He was in love with his piano teacher's daughter, Clara Wieck. But Mr. Wieck wouldn't let them be together.

Schumann wrote a song for Clara called 'Ruines' because he felt that his life was in ruins without her. That song became the beginning of the Fantasy."

Oh my *God*, how romantic. But I probably shouldn't say that to a teacher. "That's insanely interesting. How do you know this?" I ask instead.

"Conservatory. You'll see for yourself, next year."

Conservatory. I drop my gaze and study my nails.

"At Juilliard or Curtis or wherever you decide to go, you'll learn everything there is to know about the lives of the composers. Who was in love with whom, who died of syphilis at age thirty-one, who had a morbid fear of the number thirteen . . ." Mr. Rossi hesitates, apparently noticing that I've checked out on this conversation. "You *are* a senior, right? That's what it said on my class roster: 'Beatrice Kim, senior.' "

I nod.

"Sorry . . . I simply assumed . . . So you're *not* applying to conservatory, then?"

"Nope."

"It's just that I don't run across people your age who can play the Schumann Fantasy like that. Or at all. You have 'piano performance major' written all over you."

"Thanks. Actually, I was thinking more along the lines of . . . um . . ." *Quick, make something up.* "Pre-law."

"Pre-law?"

My phone buzzes. I glance at the screen. It's a text from Plum: *I'm done. Where are you? Meet me out front.*

"I have to go," I say, rising to my feet.

Mr. Rossi glances at his watch. "Actually, so do I. I'm due at a meeting that starts—started—five minutes ago. It's probably not good to keep Principal Oberdorfer waiting."

"See you in class, then."

"Yes. See you in class," he replies. "Beatrice?"

"Yes?"

"The rest of the Schumann. Could I hear you play it sometime?" He sounds shy and hesitant, like he's asking me out. My heart feels hot and fluttery.

"I'm still working on it," I murmur.

"Good. I can offer you more unwanted advice, then." He smiles, and I have no idea if he's joking or not.

I'd better start working extra hard on that last movement.

SEVEN

"Have you ever been friends with a teacher?" I ask Plum.

We are sitting on her bed getting ready to take the verbal section of a practice SAT test. A bowl of grapes, a plate of warm shortbread cookies, and two mugs of Earl Grey tea are on a tray between us. Plum's phone is set to timer mode, and she has sharpened about a hundred pencils.

"A teacher? Not really," Plum replies as she reaches for her tea. "No, that's not true! I was bored at my old school—Dad called it 'underchallenged'—so he and Mom arranged for this college TA guy, Marcus, to tutor me privately. Marcus was supposed to make me read *Finnegan's Wake* and stuff like that. But most of the time we'd just get Starbucks and talk about our favorite TV shows."

"Sounds fun."

"It was! Why are you asking? Wait, is this about Kit Harington?"

I attempt a casual shrug. "I kind of hung out with him today, after school. Well, not hung out, exactly, but had a conversation with."

"I *knew* it!"

"Knew what?"

"You like him," Plum says with a sly smile.

"Seriously, *no*. He may be cute, but he's also old. And a teacher. He's super smart about music, that's all."

"If you say so." Plum picks up two identical pencils, compares them, and sets one down. "He's technically a sub, right? He's here because Mrs. Singh had her twins this summer."

Mrs. Singh. I have a vague memory of the old music history teacher who was also in charge of the student orchestra and several chamber groups. I can picture her at the spring concert, the curve of her ginormous belly barely camouflaged under a maternity outfit. "When is Mrs. Singh coming back?"

"I'm not sure. I heard a rumor that she might not come back at all. So maybe your Mr. Rossi is going to be permanent?"

"He is not my Mr.—"

"Hey, I just had *the* best idea! You should ask him for a letter of recommendation. I bet he'd write you a really fantastic one, since you're a musical genius. *Plus,* he's your new best friend."

"He is not my new—"

"You'd still need another rec letter, though. Let's see, what about Mr. O'Donnell? Or Ms. Nargi? I think she went to Harvard, so her name may mean something there."

"Fine, whatever. I'll get right on it."

She gives me a funny look but doesn't say anything more. We turn our attention to our practice tests. I can feel Mr. Rossi's handkerchief bunched up in my pocket, pressing against my hip bone. For some reason, it makes me really happy; it's like a shiny secret that makes the rest of the world seem less dull. Still, I wonder if I should try to put it back where I found it.

As Plum starts her phone timer, I grab a cookie and read the first question:

> Serena had never been to Paris, but she could experience the City of Lights _____ through her friend Paul's lively anecdotes.
>
> (A) secretly
> (B) insufficiently

(C) vicariously

(D) gradually

(E) mysteriously

I choose option C. In the margin I copy the word "vicariously" in frilly cursive. Next to it I draw a picture of a grand piano covered with a tangled morass of rose vines. I add a pair of sexy lips. Under the piano I write: *secretly, insufficiently, gradually, mysteriously.*

Plum catches sight of my doodles.

"What are you doing?" she whispers.

"Plum, you don't need to whisper."

"What are you doing?" she repeats, more loudly. "We have to pretend we're really taking the SATs, so no doodling! And get busy!"

"Yes, Dictator Mom."

The next question has to do with the Battle of Hastings. As I fill in the answer, it occurs to me that I'm strangely relieved that Mrs. Singh might not return to school and that Mr. Rossi might become permanent. Not that I care about what happens after I graduate, but still. At least for the near future, I'll have something to look forward to: playing the Schumann Fantasy for him, talking about music. Seeing that gorgeous face.

Am I crazy, or does he act like a guy around me instead of a guy/teacher?

I'm crazy.

By the time Plum's phone timer beeps at us with its chirpy cricket ringtone, I have completed this section of the test and covered the blank pages with more rose vines.

"Yes! Finished!" Plum announces happily. "I think I got them all right. What about you?"

"Maybe. Okay, now *Buffy*."

"Let's add up our scores first."

"You really are a Dictator Mom."

"I know. One of us has to be!"

We check our answers against the key in silence. The smell of Swedish food wafts up from the kitchen: meatballs, beets, and Jansson's Temptation, which was named after a monk who broke his fast. I mean, who wouldn't give in to sliced potatoes baked in a gallon of cream? Mr. Sorenson is cooking tonight, as he always does on Tuesdays when he isn't busy designing museums or rich people's houses.

It turns out that I got all the answers right except for one, about Vladimir Nabokov. I never liked his novels, anyway. Plum said we have to score 2200 or better when we take the real test in October. I guess this is what we need if we want the Ivies to even consider our applications.

I glance down at my SAT practice test and trace the rose vine doodles with my finger. Where will I be a year from now? College? Still in Eden Grove? Or is there some unknown destiny that will secretly, gradually, and mysteriously reveal itself to me?

And then the beginning of the Schumann Fantasy flits through my mind.

I wonder whatever happened to Robert Schumann and his piano teacher's daughter?

I start a new list in my head: *Things to Talk About with Mr. Rossi.*

EIGHT

On Wednesday, Mr. Rossi catches my eye as I'm leaving his class.

"Beatrice, do you have a second?" he calls out.

"Sure!" I push my backpack up my arm as I wait for him to continue. He gives me That Smile, and I swear, he seems really happy to see me. Like he was waiting all of eighth period for this. I know that *I* was, listening to him lecture about Bach and not being able to think about anything except how his sexy stubble would feel against my face.

I really need to rein this in.

Several students bump into me as they hurry into the hallway. Mr. Rossi touches my elbow lightly and eases me away from the door.

His hand is still on my elbow when the room clears. I should probably move away, but I don't. Neither does he.

I choreograph the conversation we are about to have:

Mr. Rossi (caressing my cheek): I've been think-
ing about you.

Me (smiling seductively): Really? I've been
thinking about you too. . . .

"You have something in your hair." Mr. Rossi reaches over and plucks a candy wrapper. "Tootsie Roll. You don't see these much in Britain."

A Tootsie Roll wrapper? *God*, how embarrassing. How did it even get there? And then I remember Plum offering me a piece before history class.

He smooths back a lock of my hair. "There. Sorry, I didn't mean to mess up your . . . Anyway, I wanted to ask you: How do you feel about Rachmaninoff?"

He touched my hair. "Rachmaninoff?" I squeak.

"Yes. The Russian composer."

"I know who Rachmaninoff is."

"Yes, of course you do. I didn't mean—"

"No, it's . . . um . . . I love his music. In fact, I'm working on his 'Little Red Riding Hood' étude now. You know, the repeated-notes-and-jumping-chords étude. Plus, I've always wanted to learn his second sonata."

"Those are great pieces. But I didn't mean his solo music.

I meant his chamber music. Specifically, his Piano Trio in G Minor. Do you know it?"

"His Piano Trio in G Minor?" I scrunch up my face, trying to remember. "Is that the one that starts—" I hum a few notes.

"That's the D minor. The G minor goes like this." He crosses the room in three quick strides, leans over the piano, and plays several measures.

"No, I've never heard that one."

"Rachmaninoff composed it when he was nineteen, in memory of Tchaikovsky. There's a video on YouTube, with Vadim Repin on violin, Lang Lang on piano, and Mischa Maisky on cello. I'll e-mail you the link. So would you be interested?"

"Would I be interested in . . . what?"

"In performing it. I already have a violinist and cellist. We just need a pianist. The piano part is quite difficult, and I didn't think there was anyone here who could pull it off, but then I heard you yesterday . . . " His voice trails off as he waits for my response.

"Um . . . " I hesitate, unsure of how to explain. "The thing is, I'm not a real pianist. "

"That's very amusing."

"What I mean is, I'm not a real pianist *these days*. I'm not taking lessons with, you know, Mrs. Lugansky, and I don't have the time to learn new repertoire. I'm supposed to be studying for my SATs and filling out college applications and—"

"I assure you, this will not take up more than a few hours a week of your time. We're planning on meeting Tuesdays and Thursdays after school. In fact, we're going to meet tomorrow. Can you join us, just to see what it's like? You won't be able to learn the piano part by then, but the three of you could at least read through it together and break it down."

His eyes fix on mine. I never noticed the color of them before; they are blue and gray and green, like the ocean.

I try to collect my thoughts. *What to do, what to do . . .*

"It would be great to work together," he adds.

"Really?"

"Yes. It's . . . um . . ." He stuffs his hands into his pockets. "It's a rare thing to meet a pianist of your caliber, especially at the high school level."

"Um . . ." I'm so flustered by his remark that I can barely form an answer. Not the "pianist of your caliber" remark, but the "It would be great to work together" remark. *What did he mean by that?*

"Can I see the score first?" I say, finally.

His face lights up. "Of course! You can have my copy. And I'll let Braden and Lianna know you're tentatively on board."

"I'm not promising anything," I say hastily. "Wait, did you say Braden?"

"Yes. Braden Hunt. He's an excellent cellist."

I frown. *Braden.* This could be awkward.

I consider making up a quick excuse: *I'm sorry, I totally forgot that I have this other thing on Tuesdays and Thursdays.* But Mr. Rossi is already reaching into his brown leather messenger bag and digging around for the score. "I jotted down my preferred fingering in the more virtuosic sections. But please feel free to substitute it with your own, especially since your hands are much smaller than mine."

My gaze falls on his hands. They're wide and strong with long, slender fingers. He can probably do tenths and maybe even elevenths with complete ease.

"Beatrice?"

"I'm sorry—what?"

"I said, if all goes well, the three of you would be closing the holiday concert with this piece."

"Yes, okay."

Working with Mr. Rossi. I wonder what I'm getting myself into.

NINE

I skip dinner at the Sorensons' so I can go home and practice. I hate missing make-your-own-tacos night, and Plum was disappointed; she even tried to bribe me with the promise of mani-pedis and more *Buffy*. Mani-pedis are the one shallow, girly indulgence we both enjoy, and I have to admit that my nails always look amazing after she's worked on them. But I can't show up to the rehearsal tomorrow without at least running through the Rachmaninoff a couple of times. I don't want to let Mr. Rossi down.

When I walk through the front door, I hear the dishwasher whirring in the kitchen. The air smells like Murphy's soap and tea tree oil. A moment later Hannah *clunk-clunks* down the stairs with the vacuum cleaner.

"Well, hello there, young lady! You're home early," she calls out in a cheerful voice. Her long gray hair is tied back in a loose ponytail, and she wears a baggy NYU MOM T-shirt over her paint-splattered jeans.

I'd forgotten that she'd be here today. "Hey, Hannah. How are you?"

"Can't complain. I stopped by Wegmans and picked up some groceries for the two of you. Cleaned out the refrigerator too. I found some takeout Thai that may have been in there since Christmas."

"Oh, wow. Sorry."

Hannah has been our housekeeper since forever. When I was little, I was really taken with the fact that Nancy Drew had a housekeeper named Hannah too—and also a lawyer father and no mother. That odd little intersection of our lives used to strike me as incredibly profound, especially since my set of Nancy Drews belonged to my mom. Her name is in all the inside covers, *Natalia Levin*, in super-curly cursive with hearts over the *i*'s. If she were anyone else, I would totally make fun of the tween princess handwriting.

I sit down at the piano, set my backpack on the floor, and warm up with a couple of scales. Fortunately, it's cool to play in front of Hannah. Cream Puff appears out of nowhere and propels herself onto my lap.

"That kitty-cat tried to help me sweep the hallway. Is

he a guest or permanent?" Hannah picks up a glass from the coffee table, sniffs, and makes a face.

"*She.* I'm not sure. Permanent, I hope," I reply.

"Every stray in this town is onto you, missy. Soon they'll all show up at the door expecting room and board."

"Dad would have a stroke."

"Your father likes cats more than you realize."

"Yeah, I don't think so."

I feel Hannah giving me a look, but I don't meet her eyes. I run through the rest of my scales and then my arpeggios. Finally, I'm ready to tackle the Rachmaninoff. Hannah has disappeared into the kitchen and is emptying the dishwasher with a lot of banging and clattering.

I open Mr. Rossi's score and set it down on the music rack. The piece is in the key of G minor, which means two default flats: B flat and E flat. Mozart used G minor to express his serious, tragic mode versus his light, cheery, skipping-through-a-field-of-daisies mode. Much of Verdi's *Requiem,* which is epic and awesome, is in G minor.

I leaf through the pages and pore over Mr. Rossi's markings. His handwriting is small and precise and elegant, although in a few places he has written phrases like EMPHASIZE CHORD and EMOTIONAL LOW POINT in large, agitated capital letters, as though he was in the throes of some particularly manic practice session.

I try some of his fingerings. My mind drifts, and I picture him sitting at his piano playing the same notes I am playing. Did he use a light touch here? A heavy touch there? Did he play this in high school too? When was that? And where?

And just what did he mean, "emotional low point"? Was he going through something traumatic when he wrote that, like a depression or a breakup or a—

Focus, I tell myself.

I pick up a pencil and lightly cross out some notes I can't reach. Because I have small hands, I have to cheat the original music, which means dropping or rolling notes as creatively and unobtrusively as possible.

After I'm done marking up the score, I run through the piece very, very slowly from beginning to end. I want to get it just right before I play it for Mr. Rossi. At some point I'm vaguely aware of Hannah kissing the top of my head and saying, "I left you a lasa gna on warm" . . . and Cream Puff jumping off my lap in search of dinner . . . and the room growing twilight-dark. I bend into the light of the gooseneck piano lamp and run through the piece a second time closer to tempo . . . then a third time just under tempo.

Dad walks through the door right in the middle of the *tempo rubato* section.

I stop abruptly and slap the score shut. It flops and slides down onto the keyboard. "I was just about to fix myself something to eat. Are you hungry?" I ask quickly.

"I, um, already ate." He looks confused, disoriented. "Bea?"

"Yes. It's me, Dad."

"You sounded just like—"

He stops and shakes his head. He's acting like I'm a ghost.

"Hannah was here," I rush on in a too-bright voice as I shove Mr. Rossi's score into my backpack. "She said hi. She cleaned out the fridge. I think she left us a lasagna too. How is your trial going?"

I wait with bated breath. Will Dad yell at me? Or will he simply fall into one of his impenetrable bad moods?

He rubs the bridge of his nose, then gives me a tired smile. "Yeah, the trial is a pain in the you-know-what. The judge seems partial to the prosecution on this one. He keeps granting their motions, even though they're completely without merit. I'm going to relax for a bit, and then I have to draft a brief. Do you need anything?"

"I'm good."

"College applications going okay?"

"Yup." *No.*

"And you're taking your SATs when?"

"First Saturday in October." Which *would* have been a lie, except that Plum went ahead and registered me.

"Great, great."

I head upstairs. Crisis averted. I decide I'll change into my pj's, grab a piece of lasagna after, and eat it at the breakfast bar while I do my English homework.

My room is pitch-black. I snap on a light and see that Hannah has been here. My bed is made, and my teddy bear, Ludwig—short for Ludwig Van Bear-thoven—sits up perkily against freshly plumped pillows. My floor is clear of clothes and the usual random clutter. My Nancy Drews are lined up just so on the ancient blue shelves with the faded sea horse appliqués on them.

When I come back downstairs a few minutes later, Dad is sitting on the couch staring at CNN and cradling a scotch in his hands. There is just a wisp of amber left in the glass. A pretty blond journalist teleprompts about the situation in the Middle East. Cream Puff jumps up and rubs up against him, but he doesn't seem to notice her.

When he sucks down the rest of the scotch, I can almost see the muscles in his jaw grow soft.

"God damn it," I hear him mutter quietly.

Crisis not averted after all.

I tiptoe into the kitchen and close the door behind me.

Maybe I should find somewhere else to start practicing.

TEN

Braden and Lianna are already in the music history room when I show up for our first rehearsal. They stand at the Steinway with their backs to me as they tune their instruments.

Lianna tucks her violin under her chin and plays an A on the piano. When she follows with an A on her violin, it groans and modulates flat.

"Awful," she declares as she adjusts a string. "It's all this rain and humidity."

"Tell me about it," Braden agrees, gliding his bow across his cello. "I had a studio recital last weekend, and I couldn't play two measures without falling out of pitch."

I enter the room and slide my backpack down my shoulder. They both turn.

"Bea Kim!" Lianna smiles and waves her bow at me. "Long

time no see, sweetie. Dane told us that you'd be joining our little group."

"Dane?"

"That would be Mr. Rossi. Some of us are on a first-name basis," Braden says, slanting a look at Lianna.

"Oh!" *So his first name is Dane.*

I'd forgotten how pretty Lianna is—like Audrey Hepburn with a super-tall ballerina's body. Today she is retro-stylish in a pink sweater set, gray pencil skirt, and flats. Her only makeup is a streak of bright red lipstick, which pops against her pale white skin. She has a large purplish bruise on her neck, and then I remember: violin hickeys.

Braden hasn't changed much since the last time I saw him, which was earlier in the summer. He is still earnest-looking and just shy of hot, with his curly ginger hair and short rugby-player build. Although he can be *very* hot at times—say, when one happens to be drunk on a bottle of wine that one borrowed from a parent's liquor cabinet. But I suppose Braden could say the same about me.

I hope it's not going to be uncomfortable, us playing together.

"What happened to the science-nerd glasses?" Braden asks me casually.

"Contacts."

"And your hair . . . you did something . . ."

"It's just longer. I'm too lazy to get it cut. Where's Mr. Rossi?" I ask, glancing around.

"Dane said that he'd be here in a few minutes and that we should get started," Lianna volunteers.

"Fine with me." I pull Mr. Rossi's score out of my backpack and sit down at the piano to warm up. What's with this "Dane" business, anyway?

"I didn't know you played piano," Braden says to me. "Mr. R said he just gave you your part yesterday. If you want, we could read through this at half tempo."

"I can do tempo," I reply.

Braden blinks. "Tempo, seriously?"

"If I can't keep up, I'll drop the left hand or whatever," I assure him.

"Wow, okay. If you say so. You never mentioned you're a musician."

"Yeah, well. It never came up."

He and Lianna finish tuning while I run through a bunch of scales. And then we're ready to go. They scoot their folding chairs closer to me and set their scores on black metal stands that have the initials *AJH* written on them in silver marker. I arrange my score on the music rack, first bending and massaging the spine so the pages will be easy to turn.

I place my hands on the keyboard and peer at Lianna. She positions her violin and bow and gives me a slight nod. Braden nods too.

After a beat Braden inhales loudly and dips his head toward his bow arm. Then he begins to play. A measure later Lianna joins him. Their duet is a mere whisper because the music is marked *ppp,* for *pianissimo possible,* which means "softest possible."

I jump in at the fourth measure, at *p,* which is simply *piano* or "soft." The shift from *ppp* to *p* is subtle and sublime, especially with the three voices weaving together. I've never played chamber music; I've never even performed in public, except for Plum a couple of times, and of course the various people who've overheard me practicing: Dad, Hannah, Mr. Rossi. Grandma Min, when she used to visit us from Tucson. I have to admit, it's really amazing to create sound with other instruments.

We play on. The initial rush of pleasure begins morphing into sheer hard work. I have to focus, really focus, to execute my part. Despite the hours of practice last night and my stellar sight-reading skills, the piece is still unfamiliar and not in my body yet. It will be, though, eventually. By the holiday concert I should be able to run the entire thing from muscle memory— if I stay in this group, that is.

The piece accelerates. Halfway through the *appassionato*

section, which is fast and frantic, my left hand shoots out to turn the page as my right hand flies across the keyboard. But someone beats me to the page-turning—Mr. Rossi. How long has he been standing there?

I'm rattled but manage to play on. Mr. Rossi continues to page-turn for me. He knows the piece so well, and the rhythm of my playing so well, that he turns each page at the precise millisecond without waiting for my signal. It's almost like we're playing the piano part together.

After the *appassionato* section comes the *tempo rubato* section, then the *risoluto*.

As the piece reaches its climax, it swells and then settles. Slowly, gradually, the music trickles back down to *p*, then *pp*, then *ppp*.

The violin and cello fade away, and the last two measures of the piece are mine alone: three G-minor chords, each more quiet than the last. With the final chord, I come down as lightly and tenderly as I can and then hold . . . and hold . . . and hold.

When I finally let go, I can feel Mr. Rossi watching me as I sink my trembling hands onto my lap.

Silence fills the room.

We all glance up at Mr. Rossi. He is still watching me.

"Well?" Lianna's voice slices through the stillness.

Mr. Rossi startles as though waking up from a trance. "What? Sorry. Yes, it's a good beginning."

Lianna pouts. "A good beginning? That's all?"

"This is your first time together. Beatrice, I thought you didn't know this piece."

"I didn't. I learned it last night."

"Last night." For a moment Mr. Rossi seems at a loss for words. Lianna whispers something to Braden.

"Right, then. Why don't we take it from the top?" Mr. Rossi finally manages.

This time he pulls up a chair to the left of me, which is the usual protocol for a page-turner. When I play the opening octaves, he leans in so closely that I can feel his warm breath on my neck.

My pulse quickening, I give in to the music.

63

ELEVEN

That night when I get home, I log on to my computer and find an e-mail from Mr. Rossi:

> I need to discuss an important music-related matter with you. We could meet tomorrow after school in my classroom, if you are free. I'll also be at Café Tintoretto Saturday afternoon from around 4:00 to 6:00, if that's more convenient. Just 30 minutes, I promise.
>
> Dane

At the bottom of the message is his phone number.

I read the e-mail again—twice, three times, four times. What does it mean?

I go get my phone downstairs to call Plum. I need to talk to her immediately. An imaginary flirtation was one thing. But this . . .

"How was your chamber rehearsal thingy?" she says as soon as she picks up. "Also, do you want to come over for dinner? Like, seven? Daddy and I harvested all the basil from the garden because he said there might be a hard frost soon. We made pesto!"

"Pesto sounds great, but I can't. Listen, I . . . Mr. Rossi e-mailed me," I blurt out.

"About what?"

"He says he wants to discuss something music-related with me. Here, listen." I read the e-mail out loud.

"Oooh, a *date*!" she shrieks when I'm finished.

"Plum, it's *not* a date."

"Definitely go with Saturday. Tell him tomorrow is out because, you know, your Dictator Mom best friend is forcing you to come over for an SAT prep session."

"Oh, yay."

"You'll thank me when you get a perfect score. You're going to say yes, right? To the café invite?"

"Sure, I guess so."

"What are you going to wear?"

"What difference does that make?"

"Wear your red top—you look really sexy in it."

"Plum!"

I hear her cackling on the other end. *Witch.* I flop down on the living room couch and stare up at the ceiling. Cream Puff jumps onto my chest and digs in her claws.

And then Plum is talking again, not about Mr. Rossi but the other thing. College.

"We're all set for Columbus Day weekend! I signed us up for a Harvard information session and tour on Saturday morning. They were *literally* the last slots available for the whole weekend! I also signed us up for Northeastern and Tufts. We have some time on Sunday and Monday if there are other colleges you want to visit, like maybe MIT and BU? Oh, and Aunt Jessika said we can stay with her and her girlfriend at their town house. Isn't that great? They have four cats! Your dad said it was okay, right? And make sure you get out of your lesson with Scary Russian Lady. You and I have never been on a road trip together. It's going to be so much fun. . . ."

After rambling about college some more, Plum announces that she has to go. We blow kisses over the phone and hang up. I shake Cream Puff off my chest and head back upstairs to my computer.

Sitting down at my desk, I try to compose a reply to Mr. Rossi. Do students and teachers hang out in cafés? I remember that Mr. Starmer used to hold "office hours" at The Grind on Friday afternoons. But he was really old and sort of a famous poet, so people expected him to act eccentric. I remember, too, seeing Mr. Jablonski and Annie Richmond there once, talking quietly in a corner. There was a rumor that they were having an affair, but nothing ever came of that, and Annie ended up dropping out of school because she got pregnant— not with Mr. Jablonski's baby, but with some random JV basketball player's baby.

I guess it can't hurt to meet Mr. Rossi at this Café Tintoretto place. Because I'll only stay for a minute. Or thirty minutes. Whatever.

I type:

Dear Mr. Rossi,

Wait . . . he's "Dane" now.

Dear Dane,

Who starts an e-mail with "Dear"?

Thank you for your note. Tomorrow doesn't work, but it happens that I'm free around 4 p.m.

on Saturday, so I will stop by Café Tintoretto
then. If anything comes up last minute, here is
my cell . . .

Too businesslike.
I stare at the blank screen for what seems like forever.
Finally, I type:

Yes, Saturday, Café Tintoretto at 4.

Simple and unambiguous.
I add my phone number as a P.S. and hit Send.
Now there is no going back.

TWELVE

On Saturday, I rush into Café Tintoretto at ten minutes past four. It's on a tiny side street and not easy to find. The inside is small and dimly lit, with stained-glass windows, high tin ceilings, and a handful of antiquey tables. Gold-framed paintings of Greek gods and goddesses cover the orange walls. A scratchy but beautiful rendition of the "Flower Duet" from the opera *Lakmé* spins on an ancient record player.

I am wearing the red top Plum likes, but only because it's laundry day and nothing else is clean.

Mr. Rossi—Dane—jumps to his feet when he sees me. When I reach his table, we stand there awkwardly for a second; do we shake hands or what?

"I—," I begin.

"I—," he says at the exact same time.

We both smile. "Sorry, you go ahead," he says.

His gaze lingers on my face. Does he notice that I'm wearing makeup for once? Although "makeup" might be an exaggeration, since it's just a new lip gloss color, Naked Peach, and an invisible layer of blush. I tried eye shadow as well, but it looked too obvious, so I baby-oiled it off.

"I just wanted to say, this is my first time here. It's nice."

"Yes, isn't it? It's rather an anachronism."

Dane is in weekend mode in a gray cashmere sweater, jeans, and tortoiseshell glasses. The sweater looks impossibly soft, and I have to resist the urge to touch it; that would definitely not be cool.

A sleek silver laptop sits on the table next to a pile of scores. Stickers cover the lid: ASPEN MUSIC FESTIVAL, TANGLEWOOD, ROYAL ACADEMY OF MUSIC, CONSERVATOIRE DE PARIS.

"Lesson planning," he says, nodding at the scores. "I've found this to be a good place to get work done. It's often empty this time of day."

I point to one of the scores. "'Suite from Cinderella'? What's that?"

"It's a suite by Prokofiev, arranged for two pianos. Fantastic piece. You know, you and I should play it together sometime."

"Really?"

"Really. The orchestra room has two pianos, so we could rehearse there."

Dane and me playing "Suite from Cinderella" together . . .
the thought of it makes me strangely giddy. And it's not just the
prospect of having lots of practice sessions with him alone. The
chamber rehearsal on Thursday made me realize how nice performing with other people can be. With Lianna and Braden, it
was great. With Dane, it would be . . . epic.

He is asking me a question.

"I'm sorry, what?" I say.

"I haven't ordered yet. Can I get you something?"

I hesitate. I was only going to stay for a short while.

I glance around; there's no one else from A-Jax here, which
is no surprise, since everyone goes to The Grind. The only
other customers are a couple in the corner who are discreetly
making out. I try not to gawk at them.

"Um, sure. Yes. Thank you," I say quickly.

Dane smiles at me—not his usual devastating smile, but
a shy, eager smile—and for a moment I swear he looks like a
teenager and not a teacher. What is that about? He seems different outside of school: friendlier, less guarded.

We walk over to the marble counter together. Behind it an
old man in an apron pours foamy milk into a white cup while a
strange-looking silver urn hisses and sputters steam.

"*Ciao, Professore!*" he booms jovially at Dane.

"*Ciao, Signor Vitale. Come stai?*" Dane replies.

"Bene, bene. E tu?"

"Bene, grazie."

Dane pulls out a slim black wallet and turns to me. "Beatrice, what would you like?"

"You speak Italian?" I ask, surprised.

"I'm Italian on my father's side. How do you feel about cappuccinos?"

"I feel fine about cappuccinos. Wow, so you're bilingual."

"Actually, I speak four languages. Not because I'm brilliant or sophisticated, mind you. I was forced to take French and German at my school, and I hated every minute of it. Also, we traveled quite a bit. *"Due cappuccini, per favore,"* he says to Signor Vitale.

"Si, arriva subito."

We? I wonder if he's talking about his family growing up or about a family now. I sneak a glance at his left hand. Still no wedding ring. Also, *traveled,* past tense.

We take our cappuccinos back to the table. The make-out couple gets up to leave, their arms snaked around each other. Dane glances at them and then at me. He rakes a hand through his hair and clears his throat. "So."

"So."

"What are you working on these days?"

"You mean, like, music?"

"Yes, I mean, like, music."

"Well, there's the Rachmaninoff and the Schumann Fantasy, obviously. I'm also working on the Beethoven Opus 111, 'Jeux d'eau,' and some other stuff: Bach, Chopin . . . oh, and Prokofiev, speaking of."

"Which Prokofiev?"

"The sixth sonata."

"Ah, yes, the first of the three War Sonatas."

"War Sonatas?"

"He wrote them at the onset of World War Two. They were a reaction to Stalin, whose secret police arrested and shot his friend. Have you gotten to the third movement yet? It's quite lyrical and romantic, in contrast to the other movements which are quite . . . well, violent."

"I'm only on the first movement. It's seriously difficult."

"Has your Mrs. Lugansky pointed out the conflict between the A-major and A-minor keys?"

Mrs. Lugansky. "N-no."

"It gives the piece a very tense, unstable mood. Have you picked up on that?"

"Yes, now that you mention it."

We sip our cappuccinos. It's incredibly delicious—strong, sharp coffee with an airy layer of warm milk. Sunlight streams through the stained-glass window above us and ornaments our table with flecks of ruby, emerald, and sapphire. I touch one of the rubies, and my hand glows red.

"Beatrice?"

"Yes?"

"Listen, the reason I asked you to meet with me . . . the thing is . . . okay, I'll just say it. Why do you want to major in pre-law?"

"Excuse me?"

"You mentioned the other day that you were thinking of pursuing pre-law at university. Why?"

"Well . . . um . . ."

His ocean eyes flit across my face as he waits for my response. *This* is what he wanted to talk to me about? And how am I supposed to answer? *I have zero interest in pre-law, it's just something I made up to explain why I'm not going to be a piano performance major. Ever.*

"My dad is a lawyer. I think I'd be good at it too," I say, improvising.

"I see. What kind of law does your father practice?"

"Mostly criminal defense."

"Is that what you'd like to specialize in? Criminal defense?"

"I'm not sure. Maybe?"

"And what does your mother do?"

"My mom is . . . she passed away."

Dane gives a start. "Oh! I'm very sorry. I had no idea."

"That's okay. It's pretty much ancient history."

"Yes, but still . . ."

He sits back in his chair and gazes pensively out the window. How did we get on this subject? I don't talk about my mom often, or ever—not even with Plum.

"Beatrice?"

"What?"

"I hope I'm not speaking out of school. It's just that I've never met anyone like . . . anyone your age with so much musical potential. You belong at a conservatory, not a regular college. You have a great future as a pianist, if you choose to go that route."

You have a great future as a pianist. No one has ever said those words to me before. For a fleeting moment I'm insanely pleased, before the warning bells start going off in my brain.

"Hasn't your Mrs. Lugansky told you as much? Surely, she's offered to advise you on conservatories and help you prepare your applications?" Dane goes on.

I fold and unfold my napkin, which has *Café Tintoretto* printed on it in gold cursive. I take a few deep breaths to try to quell my growing anxiety. If only I'd taken photography with Mrs. Lutz instead.

But then I might have never met Dane.

"There is no Mrs. Lugansky," I confess.

"Sorry . . . what?"

"There is no Mrs. Lugansky. I don't have a piano teacher. I've never had a piano teacher."

"You're not . . . are you telling me you're *self-taught*?"

"Yes. From books and online and stuff. I invented Mrs. Lugansky a long time ago."

"Why in the world would you do such a thing?"

I fold my arms across my chest defensively. "I didn't want to tell people that I taught myself piano because . . . well . . . how you reacted just now. It makes me sound like a complete freak. So I created a fictional piano teacher." I don't add that sometimes lies just come out of my mouth for no good reason, and then I have to tell more and more lies for maintenance purposes. I also don't mention the thing about my mom and dad.

"You're self-taught," Dane says with a stunned expression. "Do your parents . . . I mean, does you father . . . is there some reason why he didn't enroll you in lessons when you were a child?"

"It's complicated."

His brow furrows. He seems to be considering something.

"Listen. Beatrice. I'd like you to play for someone I know," he says after a moment.

"Someone who?"

"My teacher. My former teacher. I can ring her and ask her if she would be willing to hear you."

"Does she live around here?"

"No, she lives in New York. She's on the faculty at Juilliard."

"Juilliard?"

The warning bells are going crazy now. *God.* I should never have taken music history. I should never have snuck into Dane's classroom to practice. I should never have agreed to join his little trio.

Tears well up in my eyes. I swipe at them quickly so he doesn't see.

He frowns, alarmed. "Did I say something wrong?"

"No, of course not. I have to run now. Thanks for the coffee."

I stand up to go. Dane stands up too and catches my wrist in his hand.

We stare at each other. The room disappears.

What is happening?

"I'm so sorry," he murmurs.

"Sorry for what?"

"For upsetting you. That's the last thing I wanted to do."

He moves closer, and his hand travels up my arm, leaving sparks of fire in its wake. He is a millimeter away from . . . what? Hugging me? Kissing me?

And then I feel a sudden cold void as he jerks away.

"I shouldn't have . . . I'm sorry. See you in class."

He scoops up his laptop and pile of music scores. And then he is the one to run.

THIRTEEN

Later, I'm due at Plum's for a sleepover. Actually, it's a sleepover/Common-App-essay-writing party, which was of course her idea.

As I walk to the Sorensons', my backpack slapping against my side, the air is cool and smells like moss. The leaves on the trees are beginning to tweak gold and orange. The sky is the color of metal.

My neighborhood looks different. Unreal. Hazy and shimmery, like the inside of a kaleidoscope. The cookie-cutter houses of the Pleasant Meadow development, the SUVs parked in the driveways . . . they have become interesting and even beautiful in this weirdly altered light.

I am a mess right now. Buzzy and tingly, rattled and agitated. Something has changed between Dane and me. I'm not sure what it is, but . . . *something*.

We didn't hug or kiss this afternoon at the café. He barely even touched me. But that moment we shared was more profound, more electric than anything I ever experienced with the inconsequentially few guys from my past. Andy McDermott, who I used to make out with in eighth grade, clothes on, whenever I was bored. Gil Northman, who I dated for a semester sophomore year because he was smart and funny, but whose kisses were all barbed-wire braces and peanut-butter breath. Braden, who I almost lost my virginity to over the summer—not because of love or even lust, but because I thought I should get the experience over with, and he's an okay person.

Plum always said that she and I were too good for Eden Grove boys, that we would find our soul mates when we were older and living glamorous, successful lives in some big city.

What is she going to say when I tell her about today?

Although what *is* there to say about today? How can I tell her that nothing happened and everything happened, all at once?

I've gone nearly six blocks before I realize that it's raining and that my hair and clothes are soaking wet. In fact, I've turned down the wrong street—I'm on Lake, which leads to downtown rather than to Plum's street. Are my feet retracing the way to Café Tintoretto?

Part of me wants never to see him again, *because*. And there is the Juilliard business too, which absolutely can't happen.

Another part of me wants to fall into his arms right this second. Because isn't this how two people start? A spark of attraction, a shared passion, and then one thing leads to another . . . ?

But we aren't just "two people." Also, I wonder how old he is.

This is all very complicated and confusing.

Headlights glimmer at me through the rain. A car pulls up to the curb and stops. The driver's-side door opens, and a man gets out. For a brief, wild moment I think that it's Dane. He has followed me to explain, to console me, to confess his feelings. . . .

No, not Dane.

The man circles around to the passenger side door and opens it. He holds up an umbrella as a woman gets out and teeters on high heels. He catches her in his arms, and they laugh. He starts to kiss her on the forehead, but she tips her mouth up to meet his, and they kiss for real.

Arm in arm, they cross the street and walk into a restaurant.

The sight of them makes my heart hurt. They seem to have figured out this relationship thing—this *love* thing—and right now I feel as though I will never, ever comprehend it. How do people *know*? What is it that I feel for Dane, exactly? Is it a dumb crush? Daddy issues? Am I flattered by his attention? Desperate for someone to encourage my piano playing? Or am I genuinely drawn to his intelligence and talent and kindness?

Or is love just one big, messy combination of all of the above?

FOURTEEN

As soon as I knock on the Sorensons' door, Plum flings it open and pulls me into the hallway. Shakespeare trots up to us, nails clicking against the hardwood floor, and barks dutifully at me.

"Shakespeare, be *quiet*! Bea, you didn't answer my texts. How was your date with Kit Harington?" Plum demands.

Mr. Sorenson wanders into the hallway, cradling a bowl of popcorn. He is six foot six and towhead-blond, a veritable Nordic god.

"Kit Harington? Who had a date with Kit Harington?"

Plum sighs. "No one, Daddy! It's just a joke!"

"Yes, of course it is. I apologize for my obtusity—or is it obtuseness? Hello there, young Beatrice, how goes the pursuit of truth?"

I never know quite what he's talking about; also, he pronounces my name the Italian way, *Bee-ah-tree-chay*, even though

I'm half Korean and half Ukrainian and zero Italian. But he's so jovial and nice that I don't mind any of it. "Fine, thanks, Mr. Sorenson. How is your work?"

"I've been commissioned to design a new museum in Los Angeles. I'm thinking of using paper tubes as building materials. Of course, they all think I'm crazy."

"You *are* crazy, Daddy!" Plum says with an eye roll.

"Lars, darling! You're going to miss the big scene!" Mrs. Sorenson trills from the living room.

"I believe that's my cue! I bid you adieu, ladies."

Mr. Sorenson drifts back into the TV room, munching noisily on popcorn. Plum hooks her arm through mine and drags me up the stairs.

Once we are in her room, she closes the door and turns to me with an expectant grin. *"So?"*

"So. I don't know. It was . . . " I drop my overnight bag on the floor and sink onto the bed. "He, um . . . there was this moment."

"What sort of moment?"

"Well, we were having this kind of intense conversation about music, and I got up to go, and he grabbed my wrist." I demonstrate. "For a second I thought he was going to kiss me or something."

"Did he?"

"No. It got awkward, and then he left."

"It *was* a date, then!" Plum cries out.

"Shhh, your parents will hear you."

"It *was* a date, then," she repeats in a hushed voice.

"I don't think so."

"Teachers don't just go around grabbing wrists and acting awkward and so forth."

I lean back against a mountain of mismatched pillows: green velvet, orange silk, Chinese calligraphy, Hello Kitty, a stegosaurus. "Maybe I misinterpreted."

"He's not married, is he?" Plum asks.

"No. Or at least I don't think so. He doesn't wear a wedding ring."

"Where does he live?"

"No idea."

"Where is he from, then?"

"England, maybe? He has a British accent, and he said this thing about Tootsie Rolls."

"Tootsie Rolls? What? Wait, you haven't Googled him yet? Beatrice Natalia Kim, what is *wrong* with you?"

"Everything?"

Sighing, Plum grabs her laptop and plops down on the bed next to me. "Okay. All right. What's his first name?"

"Dane."

She begins typing furiously. "Dane . . . R-O-S-S-I."

After a moment she slants the screen toward me. "There's a Wikipedia page on his family. Oh, and he's one of those middle-name people. His full name is Gabriel Dane Rossi."

"What? Really? Let me see."

We read the page together, our heads bent close. It says that Dane's parents and also his sister are professional musicians. His mother, Dominique Kessler, plays violin with the London Philharmonic. His father, Gabriel Aldo Rossi, is a cellist and a member of the Bella Musica Quartet, which has won a bunch of Grammys. His sister, Lisette Rossi, is an opera singer in Paris.

Holy cow.

There is a small mention of Dane: that he was born and raised in London and that he earned his bachelor's at Juilliard as a student of—I startle—Annaliese van Allstyne. Seriously? She is a famous pianist. I had no idea that she was also a professor.

The brief bio on Dane goes on to say that after Juilliard he taught here and there—private lessons and also at a prep school outside of New York City called the Greenley Academy—and gave a dozen or so concerts, mostly in Europe, mostly in places I've never heard of.

And now he's in Eden Grove.

I do some quick math. He's twenty-seven—so, ten years older than me. Nine, if you consider the fact that I'll be eighteen in December. We're not that far apart, really.

Plum points to the Greenley reference. "I know someone who goes there."

"Who?"

"Lakshmi, my neighbor. I guess it's a pretty fancy place. I'll have to ask her if she ever had Mr. Rossi for a teacher."

"I wonder why he left there to come to A-Jax?"

"Because he was destined to meet you, obviously."

"Obviously, ha-ha." I pick up the Hello Kitty pillow and hug it tightly. "I can't believe he thinks Annaliese van Allstyne would be willing to hear me."

"Huh?"

"At the café. That's why he wanted to meet with me. He said he wants me to play for his old teacher at Juilliard."

"You mean, like a recital?"

"No, not exactly. Like privately. Like in a lesson. People sometimes do that if they're interested in applying to a music school for college."

Plum bolts straight up, scattering pillows to the floor. "Wait a second. You're applying to Juilliard for college?" she demands in a hurt voice.

I shake my head. "No! That's my point. It would be a big, huge waste of my time."

"Okay, whew. Because I thought you liked our master plan."

"I *do* like our master plan."

"Besides, Juilliard isn't a real college, is it?"

Of course it's a real college. "Honestly, I don't know very much about it."

Plum frowns suspiciously at me. "What aren't you telling me?"

"Nothing. There's nothing I'm not telling you. Come on, let's get those Common App essays over with."

"Fine, all right. You do know that best friends tell each other everything, right? It's in the best-friend manual."

"Of course I know that. I'm not keeping any secrets from you." *Just a couple you wouldn't be interested in, anyway.*

I get my laptop from my backpack, turn it on, and fuss unnecessarily with the volume control. Even though I have good reasons to lie to Plum, I still feel a twinge of guilt. Will I ever be able to open up to her?

Maybe after a few decades of therapy.

Plum and I begin typing side by side, in silence. As I try to come up with a response to the prompt—*Discuss an accomplishment or event, formal or informal, that marked your transition from childhood to adulthood within your culture, community, or family*—my thoughts turn to Dane and his parents and sister. Why didn't he follow in their footsteps and become a big-deal musician? It's like he started to and then gave up.

Although I guess I would know something about that.

FIFTEEN

When I get home on Sunday afternoon, Dad isn't there. I grab an iced tea from the refrigerator, head upstairs to my room, and boot up my computer.

Cream Puff follows me and jumps on my lap. She smells like fabric softener, which makes me wonder if she has been napping in the laundry basket again. Hannah will not be pleased.

My screen flickers to life, and for a few minutes I mindlessly shop for new sheet music and watch a couple of YouTube music tutorials. But what I really want to do is check my e-mail to see if Dane has written. I checked on and off all night at Plum's, but . . . nothing.

I finally give in. I have half a dozen e-mails: an invitation to my cousin Jin's twenty-first birthday party, a reminder from the College Board about my upcoming SAT date, random ads. But nothing from Dane.

"Hello?"

Someone is calling up the stairs—not Dad, and not Hannah, either. I rush into the hallway to see who it is.

Peering over the banister, I stifle my surprise. It's Theo. He peels off his leather jacket, glances around for somewhere to hang it, and tosses it to the floor.

"We do have a closet," I call down to him.

He looks up with a wide grin. "Yo, Bumblebee. What's up?"

"Not much. What are you doing here?"

"Dunno. In the neighborhood. Thought I'd raid the fridge."

"Freeloader."

"Nice to see you too. Is El Padre home?"

"Nope, it's just me."

"Awesome. Come on, let's microwave some stuff. The Giants are playing."

I trot down the stairs, suddenly happy that my brother is here. He moved away to go to State when I was six. Since then, he returns to the house only sporadically, even though he lives just a few towns over.

We head into the kitchen together, and as we do, I notice the burnt-oregano smell of pot wafting from his clothes. He opens the refrigerator door and surveys the contents. "Hmm. Cheese, a can of pinto beans, salsa . . . we might be able to engineer some nachos here. How old is that pizza?"

"Um . . . Friday?"

"Outstanding. Why don't you nuke it while I look for tortilla chips? Second quarter's about to start." Theo grabs two bottles of beer, twists off the caps, and hands one to me.

"I don't like beer."

"It's time you learned. Come on, drink up."

"Jerk." I raise the bottle to my lips and take a sip. *Ugh,* it tastes like pond water.

A short while later we are sitting in the living room watching the Giants and the Broncos. Pizza, nachos, a loaf of bread, and a jar of peanut butter cover the coffee table. Also, three bottles of beer—Theo has finished his first one and is well into his second. I've managed to get through half of mine, and my head is feeling a little spinny.

Theo drapes his arm across the back of the couch, puts his feet up on the coffee table, and gives me a dazzling smile. He is really cute, and he knows it. He is also way better dressed than he should be. His leather jacket seems brand new, and his jeans and hoodie are designer. How does he afford all this on a CVS salary?

He picks up the remote and points it at the TV. "So where's the old man?"

I shrug. "I'm not sure. Maybe at the office? I just got back from a sleepover with Plum."

"What in the hell kind of name is Plum?"

"It's her nickname. She used to call herself that when she was a baby. She's my best friend, remember? Pernilla Sorenson? You met her, like . . ." I calculate. "Three Christmases ago. She came over with cookies and fruitcake."

Theo considers this. "Braces? Kind of fat?"

"She *wasn't* fat. And she's thinner now. Plus, she doesn't wear braces anymore."

"Whatever you say."

"You are such a jerk."

"Yeah, I think we already covered that." He dangles a bottle from his fingertips and takes a long swig.

We fall into an edgy silence. Theo and I always descend into this, and quickly. For the first few minutes of seeing each other, we manage to pull off a semblance of lighthearted brother-sister banter. And then our bad history takes over.

"So . . . how's life? How's Rachel?" I ask him, trying to get back to lighthearted.

"Who?"

"Rachel. The last time you were here, you said you were meeting up with your girlfriend, Rachel something."

"Oh, yeah, her. We broke up. I'm with Melissa now. She's an artist."

"That's cool. What kind of artist?"

"Dunno, paintings?"

As I reach for a nacho and nibble on an edge, I wonder if Theo has ever had a relationship that lasted longer than a few weeks. The nacho is borderline inedible. "So, um . . . how's your band? Are you guys playing gigs and stuff?"

"Not really. Our drummer just moved to New Mexico. We're looking for a replacement."

"Do you have any candidates?"

"Nope."

"Um, so, are you still working the night shift at CVS?"

"What is this, Twenty Questions? The Giants are about to score."

Obediently, I turn to face the TV. The Giants make a touchdown, and the crowd roars. Theo finishes off the rest of his beer, sets it down on the table with a loud *thunk,* and gets up. He saunters toward the front door.

"Wait! Aren't we going to watch the rest of the game?" I call out.

"I've gotta head back. Thanks for the snackage."

"Do you want to stay for dinner? I can text Dad and tell him you're here."

For a second Theo hesitates, and I feel a sliver of hope.

"Nah, don't bother. Wouldn't want to tear him away from saving criminals."

He gives me a little salute, scoops up his leather jacket, and takes off.

The sliver of hope vanishes.

The halftime show blares on the TV: a row of smiling, spray-tanned cheerleaders and a marching band lined up like toy soldiers. I stare at the carnage of beer bottles, pizza crusts, and wilting nachos on the coffee table.

I feel tired all of a sudden. Tired and sad.

The rest of the afternoon looms like a black cloud. Maybe I should check my e-mail again. Maybe I should walk over to Café Tintoretto and see if Dane is doing more lesson planning. Maybe I should go back to Plum's house.

Whatever. I can't just sit around and wallow in how much the men in my family hate me.

Especially since they have a good reason to.

Sixteen

Dane is avoiding me.

Monday in music history, I sit in the back and doodle in my notebook per usual. Today it's Batman battling the Joker on the roof of Café Tintoretto. Outside, the pale September sky swirls with storm clouds. The day is already depressing, so why not rain?

I keep sneaking Dane looks, wondering. But he is angling his face in the other direction, toward the burnouts and football players and senior sluts, as though my side of the room doesn't even exist.

"Counterpoint is the interaction of multiple voices to create harmony," he lectures at them as he flips through a pile of index cards. "But we're not talking about notes that match or mirror each other. We're talking about notes that feel as though they are in opposition, out of sync. In fact, the term 'counterpoint' comes from the Latin phrase *pontus contra punctum,* which means 'point against point.' "

"*Habeamus coitus.* That's Latin for 'Let's hook up,' " Nelson whispers to me.

I don't even bother with a scathing reply. This is why I don't date boys my age. Now that I know Dane's background, it makes sense why he teaches this class like it's a college-level course. Most of this material is way over the heads of the A-Jax kids. He's obviously used to hanging out with the music geniuses at Juilliard, not to mention the music geniuses in his family.

"Aside from Bach, which composers are known for their use of counterpoint?" Dane asks. "Anyone?"

I raise my hand in the air. Dane does not even twitch my way. After a moment Aziza raises her hand also.

Dane turns ever so slightly, managing to include Aziza in the periphery of his visual field while leaving me, just one desk behind and one desk over, out.

"Bach!" Aziza says, looking pleased with herself.

"Aside from Bach."

"Um . . ."

Laughter ripples through the room. I raise my hand again, but Dane doesn't call on me. Instead, he turns to the blackboard and starts writing:

Beethoven (late pieces)

Schumann

Franck

Shostakovich

Stravinsky (neoclassical pieces)

Hindemith

Bartók

"In his later years Beethoven was obsessed with the fugue, which is a kind of contrapuntal, or counterpoint-based, piece that introduces and develops a specific phrase throughout in a complex, interwoven way. Schumann used heavy counterpoint in everything. . . ."

I slide down in my chair and draw a big *X* through Batman and the Joker. And Café Tintoretto. Stupid Beethoven, stupid Schumann, stupid all of them. I don't know what's going on. Or maybe I do, as in, Dane feels weird about Saturday and wants to just forget about it already.

Fine, then. I will forget about it too. I can do forgetting like nobody's business.

Maybe I should see if Braden wants to start hanging out again.

When the bell rings, I gather my stuff and make a beeline for the doorway. Dane is busy erasing his composers from the blackboard, so I doubt he even notices. I don't notice him either, or the beautiful deep blue of his shirt, or the fact that his stubble looks longer than usual. So we're even.

I pause in the hallway, not sure of where to go next. Plum has a dentist's appointment, so I have to while away an hour or so before heading over to her house for *doro wat*. I don't feel like practicing at school, because *he* might be around. I don't feel like going home first, either.

I decide to head over to Braden's locker. I find him there leafing through a calculus textbook.

"What's up, Hunt?" I call out.

He turns, and his face lights up. He closes the textbook and stuffs it into his backpack. "Hey, Bea. What are you doing in this neck of the woods? Isn't your locker in C wing?"

"No, D wing. I'm between Joshua Kidman and Kyle King, who need to work on their personal hygiene and also lose the almost-porn taped to their locker doors. Don't you have orchestra now?"

"They made orchestra an official class. Third period. Mr. R has us working on the New World Symphony, which is not fun."

"Hmm." I picture Dane leading fifty or so not-very-talented students in Dvořák. With the exception of Braden, Lianna, and a few others, the music kids at A-Jax aren't too musical, despite the whole "Campus for Baccalaureate and Performing Arts" business.

"Bea?"

"Hmm?"

"I said, what do you think of our trio?"

"Um, yeah, it's fine. It's great! I haven't decided if I'm staying with it or not, though."

"You *have* to stay."

"I don't know. I'm pretty busy."

"You're an amazing pianist. Amazing, understatement. How long have you been studying?"

"Since forever."

"Yeah, well, obviously. Who's your teacher?"

I start to say *Mrs. Lugansky*, then stop myself. "I'm kind of between teachers right now."

"Are you applying to conservatories for next year? Maybe we could compare notes. Did you know that the New England Conservatory has double-degree programs with both Tufts and Harvard? That's cool, right?" Braden peers over my shoulder. "Oh, hey, Mr. R, we were just talking about you."

I whirl around. Dane is standing there.

"Good afternoon, Braden," he says, but he is looking at me. "Beatrice, are you free? Could I speak to you?"

Oh. So I guess he's not avoiding me anymore. "Actually, I'm on my way out. I was just heading over to my locker," I fib.

"Why don't I meet you at the D wing exit, then? Say, five minutes? I'll dash over to my office and get my coat. I won't keep you."

He knows where my locker is. "Um . . . sure."

Braden's gaze bounces between Dane and me. He seems confused, which makes two of us—possibly three.

Thinking quickly, I smile at Braden and touch his arm. "I'll catch you later, okay? Maybe we can grab a coffee or something?"

I notice Dane noticing my hand and feel a stupid rush of pleasure.

"Sure, anytime. You'd better be there tomorrow," Braden says, also staring at my hand.

"Tomorrow?"

"You know, rehearsal? Our trio? Please convince her to stay, Mr. R."

"Yes, of course. Beatrice, I'll see you over there in a few minutes."

"Okay."

Dane takes off down the hall. I take off in the other direction, toward the D wing, wondering what's up.

"Good-bye to you too," I hear Braden call out.

"What? Oh, sorry. Bye, Braden!"

But my mind is already a million miles away. Or as far as the D wing exit, anyway.

SEVENTEEN

Outside, the sky is gray, and a fine, icy rain mists down. Students pour into the parking lot and disappear into cars and buses. In the distance the varsity football players set up their orange training cones and run frenzied S's around them, kicking up mud.

I lean against one of the faux-Greek columns and wait for Dane. I'm not sure if he meant for us to meet out here or in the hallway. What does he want to discuss? Is this how guys normally act around girls? Hot and cold, there and not there?

And then I remind myself: *He is not "guys."*

The doors swing open, and Dane comes rushing out, his messenger bag slung over one shoulder. He looks very British and handsome in an olive trench coat.

"Hey." I wave.

He extracts an umbrella from his bag and opens it over

my head. The umbrella is small, so we have to stand very close together. "You're getting soaked. Why don't we go back inside?" he suggests.

"Here's fine. What did you want to talk to me about?"

"Right." Dane fidgets and coughs and digs through a pocket. He pulls out a random piece of paper, stares at it, and crumples it in his fist. I watch, intrigued; I've never seen him quite this nervous.

"Listen, I want to explain about the other day. At the café," he begins.

Oh.

"I hope there was no . . . that you didn't misunderstand. You were upset, and my first instinct was to . . ." He fidgets and coughs some more. "Needless to say, it won't happen again."

Well, that was anticlimactic. I thought he liked me in a not-teacher way, but obviously, I was very wrong.

Silence gapes between us.

"Okay. Is that it?" I ask, forcing myself to sound casual.

"Yes. *No!* There is the other matter, and it's far more important. I can explain while I walk you to your car. Or do you take the bus?"

The other matter? "I walked."

"What? Please let me give you a lift, then."

"No, really, I'm—"

"Nonsense. You shouldn't be out in this dismal weather."

I take a deep breath. *It's just a ride.* "Fine."

"Right, then!"

Dane leads me to a little silver sports car and opens the passenger side door for me. I don't know much about cars, but this one looks . . . expensive. Is his family rich? Is *he* rich?

I slide in and glance around. Random CDs, travel mugs, and a crinkly map of Eden Grove cover the backseat. A paperback splays half open on the floor: *Love in the Time of Cholera* by Gabriel García Márquez.

I am in Dane's car, I think, and it's surreal because it's a piece of his private life, the life that has nothing to do with A-Jax or classes or rehearsals. Like his gray cashmere sweater, like cappuccinos, like his four languages. Although he has just put up a new wall between his private life and me, so . . . so much for that.

He hurries around to the other side and gets into the driver's seat. He shakes the rain from his umbrella and closes it.

"Is that good?" I ask, pointing to the García Márquez. It occurs to me that they both have the same first name: *Gabriel.*

"You haven't read it?"

"No."

He picks it up and hands it to me. "Well, then, you must take it home and read it immediately."

I laugh. "Immediately?"

He laughs too. "Yes, immediately. Now, where shall I drop you?"

I give him my address.

"You live just a few blocks from me. I'm on Carriage House Lane." He starts the car and pulls out of the parking lot. "So! I have some good news. I spoke to my teacher. My Juilliard teacher."

My smile vanishes. "I'm sorry, what?"

"Her name is Annaliese van Allstyne. She's—"

"I know who she is," I cut in tersely.

"I told her about you, and she said she would be happy to hear you play. She just has to get back to me about her schedule. I believe she has concert engagements in South America over the next few weeks and then in Seoul and Beijing later in October."

I don't respond.

"You'll go to New York and meet with her. You could also take a tour of Juilliard. If all goes well, and if you like it there, you'll fill out an application for next fall. I can help you."

Dread twists my stomach. I wasn't expecting this—not today, not ever. I really thought Dane would forget about it, especially after my lack of enthusiasm at Café Tintoretto.

"Beatrice?"

He is obviously puzzled by my reaction. I guess he assumed I would burst into happy tears or something.

"It's very nice of you. To talk to your teacher, I mean," I manage.

"Yes, well, I was glad to do it."

I gaze out the window. A chilly fog shrouds A-Jax and makes it look almost mysterious. We drive down School Spirit Boulevard and then turn left onto Main. As we pass that tiny side street, I look for the café, but everything is obscured by rain.

"I can't," I finally say.

"You can't . . . what?"

"Go to New York City. Play for your teacher. Apply to Juilliard."

"Why on earth not?"

"I just can't."

Dane sighs as though I were a particularly stubborn child. "One of the most important pianists in the country, in the world, has agreed to hear you. This can open doors for you in ways you never imagined. You may never get an opportunity like this again."

My brow furrows, and I slouch down in my seat. He has a point.

"Does this have something to do with your father?" he persists.

I shrug.

"I have no idea why he wouldn't allow you to have lessons as a child," he says, and he sounds angry now. "You're clearly a prodigy, and you deserve every advantage. Why don't you let me speak to him? Perhaps he doesn't understand how incredibly gifted you are, the kind of future you might have if you are given the proper—"

"She went to Juilliard," I interrupt.

"Sorry. *Who* went to Juilliard?"

"My mother."

"Your mother?"

Dane pulls over to the side of the road and stops the car. He turns and stares at me, his eyes wide and bewildered. "Why didn't you tell me this before?"

"Because, I . . . it's not something I talk about."

"What did she study there?"

"Piano performance."

"Piano performance."

He shakes his head and mutters to himself as though trying to process the information. We're parked in front of my old elementary school, which is now a "cooperative kindergarten," whatever that is. The only people around are a little girl in a ladybug raincoat and a woman who must be her mom or her babysitter. The little girl keeps running back to the playground, and the woman keeps calling out to her to please let's go home already.

"When was this?" Dane asks after a moment.

"Ages ago. Before I was born, before my brother was born."

"And you don't want to go to Juilliard because it reminds you of her."

"No, not exactly. Besides, I told you before. I want to study pre-law."

He leans back as if to study me from a distance. "I don't believe you."

"Why not?"

"Because! You were born to be a pianist. I can see it in your face when you play. Piano is your passion, your soul. You come alive when your fingers touch the keyboard."

Thanks for the motivational speech, I want to say. *Tell it to someone who cares.* But in truth, his words have mesmerized me and rendered me speechless. How does he know? How can he understand me in such a deep, intimate way when no one else has even come close?

"Look. Beatrice. You don't have to apply to Juilliard if you don't want to. Or you can apply and get accepted and choose not to go there. But you owe it to yourself to at least meet Annaliese and see the campus."

I digest all this. Yes, but . . . still *no.*

"I would be happy to accompany you. In fact, I think that would be best, given your family's . . . Anyway, I can introduce you to Annaliese and also show you around."

Wait, did he just say . . . ?

"*You* want to take me to New York City?" I say incredulously.

"Just think of it as one of your university visits. You Americans do that, don't you? Visit prospective universities in your senior year?"

I think about Plum and our upcoming Boston trip. "Y-yes."

"Great! So can I tell Annaliese that you'll meet with her?"

"Dane?"

"What?"

"Why does this matter to you so much?"

Now it's his turn to be caught off guard.

"I felt like you needed somebody," he says, almost reluctantly.

"What for?"

"To help you become the person you're meant to be." His voice is husky with emotion, the way it is when he talks about music.

Something inside of me unhinges.

Eighteen

"When did the two of you first meet?"

"In September."

"He was your teacher."

"Yes."

"Did you and he ever get together after-hours? Evenings, weekends?"

"He coached our chamber group on Tuesdays and Thursdays. He gave me some private lessons, too, to get me ready for my appointment with Annaliese van Allstyne."

"Where and when did these private lessons take place?"

"Most of them were after school, at school. A couple of times was at his house, because it was a Saturday or Sunday or something and the building was closed."

"So on these Saturdays or Sundays, were the two of you alone in his house?"

"No. My friend Plum always came with me. Pernilla Sorenson. She turned pages."

"I see. And this Annaliese . . . she's the Juilliard instructor?"

"Professor. Yes."

"Why did you have to go all the way to New York City to meet with her? Couldn't you just talk on the phone or by Skype?"

"She wanted to hear me play in person. Also, I wanted to check out the school."

"This was Mr. Rossi's idea?"

"Yes."

"These events happened over the weekend of October twelfth?"

"Yes."

"Was Mr. Rossi in New York City that weekend too?"

"Y-yes."

The detective leans forward and flips his notebook to a new page.

"Why don't you tell me about that."

Nineteen

"The entire last movement. You're too polished, too precise. Can you play it again, but this time try to lose yourself a bit?"

Dane stands on the other side of the living room and regards me over the top of his glasses. His shirt is rumpled, and his hair is more disheveled than usual. He sips at a mug of coffee—his fifth this afternoon.

We have been at this for four hours. A four-hour-long piano lesson. And from what I can tell, he intends for us to continue for another four hours.

My appointment with Annaliese has been set for mid-October, and Dane and I have decided that I will perform my Beethoven, my Bach, and the Schumann Fantasy for her. The Beethoven and the Bach we dispensed with relatively quickly. It is the Schumann that has caught us in the throes of its infinite contrapuntal loop. It is without doubt the most challenging piece I've ever played or tried to play.

Maybe I'm just not good enough. Maybe I need to down-grade to something easier, like Schumann's "Twelve Pieces for Little and Big Children." Or "Chopsticks."

"Can we take a break?" I rise from the bench and massage my knuckles. "My hands feel like gnarled old trees."

Dane smiles. "Yes, of course. I'm working you too hard. Can I get you something? Coffee, tea, a glass of water?"

"I'd love some tea, thanks."

"Back in a minute."

He heads for the kitchen, and I sink down on the couch, still massaging my knuckles. While he is gone, I check out his house. This is the first time I've ever been here. We were sup-posed to have our lesson at the school, like we've been doing these past few weeks, but it turned out the building is com-pletely locked up and deserted on Sundays. My house was out, for obvious reasons, so Dane spontaneously suggested that we have today's lesson at his place instead.

When we first arrived, there was too much awkwardness for me to take in my surroundings—no *Welcome to my home!* or *Let me give you a quick tour,* just him acting more formal and teacherly than usual as he instructed me brusquely to sit down at his Yamaha baby grand and warm up with scales. Now, as I look around, I see Dane in every detail. Shelves of books with titles like *The Lives of the Great Composers* and *Mastering Piano Technique.* Framed black-and-white photographs of famous musicians. Neat piles of scores covering an Oriental rug.

I scan for clues to his personal life—family pictures, a book of love poems, a woman's scarf draped casually on the coat tree—but there is nothing.

Not that I should care. Since that time in his car, he has been very arm's-length with me, at least in that way. Mostly, he's acting like a very intense mentor/manager, trying to prepare me for my meeting with Annaliese.

He returns from the kitchen and sets a manly gray mug on the coffee table, next to an unfinished *New York Times* crossword puzzle. He has left 3 Down blank. *Romantic collaboration,* seven letters.

Liaison, I think. Maybe before, I would have taken this to be a sign. A crossword puzzle in plain sight, a suggestive word. But I've come to see that signs don't mean anything, that their importance can be wildly inflated.

Oh, well. I guess I need a mentor/manager in my life right now, way more than a teacher/love interest.

Dane sits down next to me. I catch his familiar scent of eucalyptus and fresh soap and remember the stolen handkerchief, which is hidden away in my backpack. "I hope you like peppermint. I'm afraid it's all I have," he says.

"I love peppermint. What did you mean, lose myself a bit?"

"What? Oh, yes, the Schumann. It's the opposite of the second movement, which is supposed to be very sharp and crisp. Militaristic. With the third movement, you need to let go of all that—sleepwalk, even."

"How do I sleepwalk and play the right notes at the same time?"

"Once you know the piece well enough, your hands will automatically play the right notes. But your mind, your heart . . . you need to let them go to a deeper, more uncharted place. Wander off the map, if you will. The third movement is the culmination of Schumann's intense love and longing for his unattainable Clara."

"It is?" I feel my cheeks flush as I reach for my tea. The mug is too hot, but I don't mind; it's a welcome distraction. "How did he . . . I mean, what is it about that movement . . . so I should aim for a more romantic-with-a-little-*r* mood?" I babble stupidly.

Dane picks up his empty coffee mug and studies it. "Did I ever tell you that Schumann wrote two endings for the Fantasy?"

"What? No. Two endings?"

"An original handwritten manuscript exists in which Schumann crossed out the first ending and replaced it with a second ending. The second ending is the one most pianists play . . . the one you play."

"Why did he do that?"

"No one knows for sure. Some people believe that the first ending was too personal for him to share. It contains a secret message of love that is meant only for Clara: a harmonic interval known as a descending fifth. That descending fifth was his code for her. In the second ending the descending fifth is gone."

"So the second ending is *not* a message of love for her?" I ask, puzzled.

"The entire piece, in both incarnations, is a message of love for her. It even quotes themes from Beethoven's song cycle called *An die ferne Geliebte*—'To the Distant Beloved.' The point is, the original ending of the Fantasy was a whole other level of private. Only Clara was supposed to understand it."

We sit in silence as I sip my tea and he continues staring down at his coffee mug.

"Did they ever get together?" I ask after a while.

"Yes."

"Was it happily ever after?"

"Not exactly."

"Oh."

"Their relationship was very . . . complex. Not straightforward. That's what you must capture when you play that last movement."

Complex. Not straightforward. Intense love and longing. Unattainable.

"No problem. I can handle that," I say lightly.

We avoid looking at each other.

Twenty

"I never see you anymore," Plum complains as we walk to her house for a final SAT study session. The test is tomorrow, an all-day deal that will take place in the A-Jax cafetorium under the watchful eyes of multiple scary proctors. The trees on Lark Street blaze with red and gold, and early Halloween decorations hang in the windows: jack-o'-lanterns, silhouetted witches, tissue-paper ghosts.

"I've been crazy busy lately. I'm sorry," I apologize.

"Is it your chamber thingy? Why do you guys have to rehearse so much?"

"Because we suck," I lie. "The piece we're playing is really hard."

"Is it Kit Harington, then? Is your secret romance blossoming, and you're keeping it from me?"

"No! There is no secret romance. We had our moment at

the café, but that was it. It's back to business now." Which is not entirely a lie.

"Oh."

"Hey, you and I are going to Boston next weekend!" I say brightly. "Go, maroon! Or go, magenta! Wait, what's the Harvard school color?"

"Crimson."

"Right. Go, crimson!"

Plum frowns and turns to watch a little kid race by on his bicycle. It wobbles and then steadies. I wish I could tell her everything. About my Juilliard trip, which is happening in two weeks. About the private lessons with Dane. About all the extra practicing I've had to do, to prepare. But I can't, not until after I'm back from New York City. If nothing comes of it, then I won't even mention it to her. If something does come of it, and I change my mind about going to a conservatory . . . well, I'll *have* to tell her, obviously, and we can have a big drama about it then.

Although I can't imagine that I will change my mind.

And even if I did, like I could ever get into Juilliard.

The boy zips by on his bike again. For a second I flash back to when I learned to ride one. Dad actually taught me, over a couple of Sundays, on the rare occasions when he acted like a normal dad. When I was finally able to pedal on my own without him holding on, he took a picture with his phone. He probably deleted it by accident afterward.

When Plum and I reach her front yard, she steps gingerly across the stone path instead of hopscotching like we usually do. *Ouch.* "Are you staying for dinner? Or do you have somewhere you need to be later?" she asks glumly.

"I wouldn't miss sushi from Tokyo Palace!" I say, forcing a smile.

"You missed it last week. You've missed most of our dinners lately. Mommy's been asking where you are."

"I'm sorry."

"It was Shakespeare's birthday on Tuesday. You missed that, too."

"I'm really, really sorry."

Inside, Mrs. Sorenson is waiting for us in the hallway. "Darlings!" she wraps her arms around us and kisses our heads. "How was your day? Are you all ready for the SATs tomorrow? Bea, sweetheart, we've missed you."

"I know, Mrs. Sorenson. I'm sorry I haven't been around."

"No worries. It's such a treat to see you. Pernilla told us about your trio. We're so looking forward to hearing you at the Christmas concert!"

"The *holiday* concert, you mean," Plum corrects her. "Where's Daddy?"

"He's still in L.A. He'll be home tomorrow. Now, you girls go relax or study or whatever you want to do while I make us a fruit salad."

Mrs. Sorenson smiles and pulls her hair back with a clip as she pads toward the kitchen. Plum and I take our backpacks upstairs. Shakespeare is napping on the second-floor landing. He opens one eye, thumps his tail, and goes back to sleep.

Inside her room, Plum and I tackle a couple of SAT worksheets while listening to Adele on her computer. When "Set Fire to the Rain" comes on, I automatically think: *Key of D minor.* Mrs. Sorenson brings up a wooden bowl filled with mango slices, raspberries, and mint leaves. She hugs us again before leaving to pick up our sushi from Tokyo Palace.

Everything is the same and yet not the same. Plum is upset with me. I'm lying to her more than usual. I want things to go back to where they were, before Dane . . . but I know that's not possible, at least not until I've put this Juilliard pipe dream, detour, whatever behind me.

Telling lies used to make everything easier. Now it's the opposite. What is happening to me?

Thankfully, the mood is lighter at dinnertime. The table, set for three, is as festive as ever. Garlands of bittersweet surround clusters of white votive candles. Mrs. Sorenson lets Plum and me have some Japanese wine in tiny porcelain cups. As we eat, she tells us stories about her and Mr. Sorenson's Princeton days.

"I met him the fall of my freshman year. He was a graduate student. I was on my way to the bookstore and was just about to walk through FitzRandolph Gateway, which is one of the gates on Nassau Street, the main street. All of a sudden, your father appears out of nowhere and pulls me away. I didn't know this at the time, but it's a tradition for students to wait until graduation to exit through that gate. Otherwise, it's bad luck. I was a bit shaken up—you know, having a strange young man grab me and all that. He insisted on taking me out for coffee. The rest, as they say, is history."

As I listen, I tip back the Japanese wine, which burns pleasantly down my throat. I try to picture Plum and me at college together: sharing a dorm room, strolling across an ivy-covered campus, meeting smart boys. It's such a perfect picture, and I wish I could get excited about it.

And then I picture me in New York City, majoring in piano performance at Juilliard. Dane could visit and come to my recitals . . .

Maybe it's not a mere pipe dream after all. He has unleashed something in me—not just romantic-with-a-small-*r* yearnings, but that part of me which was hidden away and buried for so long. Music.

Plum watches me from across the table. Her eyes look sad and also a little drunk. My heart sinks; does she know? Has her best-friend sixth sense intuited that a part of me may leave her? May have already left?

TWENTY-ONE

When I get home that night, Cream Puff greets me at the door with an angry yowl, like she's way overdue for a meal. Obviously, I spaced on her breakfast this morning; I've been a bad cat-mom lately.

I head for the kitchen, clicking on lights along the way. My head is still a little fuzzy from the Japanese wine. The curtains are open, and the windows stare out at blackness: black sky, black woods, black asphalt—it's all the same in this place. The only sign that Dad may have been here earlier is a pizza box on the coffee table along with a pile of manila folders. His last trial wrapped up in late September, and he's starting a new trial now—a murder case, I think, which is rare for Eden Grove. The most exciting things that happen around here are shoplifting, domestic incidents, and once, during the Super Bowl, some old guy shooting his TV set with a hunting rifle.

In the kitchen I bang open cupboard doors in search of cat food. I find a brand-new ten-pound bag of Kitty Feast that Hannah must have picked up. Cream Puff circles my ankles as I pour the kibble into her bowl. Dad hasn't made me kick her out yet; he's probably forgotten about her existence, which is par for the course for him.

My phone buzzes with an incoming call. Dane's number flashes on the screen. I perk up and hit Talk.

"Hi!"

"Am I ringing too late?"

"No, it's fine. I'm feeding Cream Puff." I reach down to pet her, but she's way more interested in her food.

"Sorry, what is a Cream Puff?"

"She's my . . . she's a cat."

"Ah! I adore cats. My cat, Mr. Bumble, is still with us— or rather, with my family back in London. He's nearly twenty now."

"Twenty! Wow."

"So how are you?"

"I'm fine."

Actually, I'm better than fine, because Dane has never called me before. We usually just text each other to arrange for lessons and such. Talking to him on the phone, late on a Friday night, seems so intimate—even more intimate than being in his house. But I don't articulate any of this because I don't want to sound cloying. Or stupid. Or stalkerish.

"So listen, I just spoke to Annaliese. She needs to change the date of your appointment in New York. Would that be all right?" he is asking me.

"Sure."

"Great. It turns out Annaliese has to be in Texas on the nineteenth to adjudicate a competition. She's filling in for another judge. Quite by chance, one of her students had to cancel his recital next Saturday. I convinced her to meet with you then."

Next Saturday? "Wait! That day's no good. Is there another day she can see me?"

"What's wrong with the twelfth?"

"I'm going to Boston with Plum."

"You must postpone it, then."

"I can't. She's been planning this forever. We're visiting colleges."

"Sorry, you didn't mention . . . I wasn't aware that you were . . . Which colleges?"

"Like Harvard, a bunch of other schools. I don't remember exactly."

Silence.

"Beatrice, are *you* interested in those schools?"

"I don't know. Maybe?"

"*Maybe.*" Another silence. "Listen to me. You can visit Harvard and so forth anytime. But you may not get another opportunity to play for Annaliese. It's very difficult to get an audience with her. She almost canceled this meeting altogether. Needless to say, she's extremely in demand."

"But—"

"It's up to you. I can't force you to go. You must decide what your priorities are."

"Yes, but—"

"Do *you* want to go to Boston next weekend?"

I sigh.

"Beatrice?"

"Okay, fine! No, I don't want to go, except for the hanging-out-with-Plum part."

"Do you want to play for Annaliese?"

"Y-yes."

"Good. It's settled, then. I'll let Annaliese know."

We talk for a few more minutes, then hang up. I lie down on the cool linoleum tile and stare up at the ceiling fan whirring around and around. Has it always been there? Did I accidentally turn it on? Cream Puff climbs onto my stomach and settles into a meat-loaf position, purring. This is all it takes to make her happy: a bowl of Kitty Feast and a warm body. If only.

When did life get so complicated?

How am I going to tell Plum that our road trip isn't happening?

Suddenly, my excitement about the New York City trip and my whatever with Dane disappears into a black hole. All I can think about is Plum and the fact that I'm about to destroy her happiness—and maybe our friendship, too.

Do I really want to go there?

TWENTY-TWO

After the SATs, Plum and I meet in front of A-Jax so we can walk over to Sweet Temptations for hot-fudge sundaes.

"How did you do?" I ask her as we fall into step together, shivering in our matching jeans jackets. It's one of those intensely bright, sunny fall afternoons that belie how Arctic-cold it is.

"I think I did well!" Plum says, beaming. "What about you?"

"Fine. It was fine. Plum?"

"What?"

I wanted to tell her last night, on the phone. Or via a cowardly text. But I figured I should at least wait until we got through today. I didn't want to be responsible for making her get less than her coveted 2200.

"I have bad news," I announce.

Plum stops on the sidewalk and grabs my arm, her eyes

wide with worry. She is such a good friend to me. I am such a bad friend to her.

"Bea! What *is* it?"

"I don't know how to . . . the thing is . . . I have to cancel Boston."

In an instant her expression of concern morphs into devastated disappointment. I'm not a bad friend; I'm a sucky, terrible friend. "What? *Why?*" Plums asks.

"My brother. He's, um, sick."

My lies usually flow so easily, but this one sticks in my throat like wet paper. It was either a Theo medical crisis or having to put Cream Puff down. It was the best I could come up with at two a.m.

"What's wrong with him?" Plum demands.

"We're not sure. But he's getting some tests done on Friday at the hospital, and my dad wants us to be there to support him."

"Tests? Oh my gosh . . . is it . . . *cancer?*"

"No! I'm sure it's not *that* serious."

"Is it something, you know, *hereditary?*"

My chest tightens; is she referring to my mom? "No. It's probably just a virus or something. I really, really wanted to go to Boston; I still do. But my dad is insisting. I'm so sorry!"

"Of course! Oh my gosh, you don't need to apologize!"

She gives me a crushing hug. We stand there on the sidewalk, bear-hugging, wobbling a little as the bitter wind stings our eyes and faces. A small part of me is relieved because I can go to New York City now. The other part of me wants to slap the first part.

Why can't I just tell her the truth?

Tommy Vacco and one of his meathead friends walk by.

"Get a room!" Tommy calls out. He and his friend crack up.

"Neanderthals!" Plum shouts.

She hooks her arm through mine, and we start toward Sweet Temptations again.

"People can be such jerks," she says, eyeing the guys up ahead.

"Yeah, they sure can," I agree.

Like I'm in any position to judge.

I never told Plum how my mom died, or under what circumstances, so I guess she's taken to filling in the blanks herself. Obviously, she thinks Theo is suffering from an inherited disease or some other Kim family curse.

There actually *is* a family curse, and I'm responsible for it. *Me.* If I hadn't shown up, my mom would still be alive and well, living in New York City with Dad and Theo. She had a successful music career, teaching young kids and playing in chamber groups.

Then I had to be born and ruin everything.

Afterward, Dad went crazy and sent Theo and me to live in Eden Grove with Grandma Min. We didn't see him again for a long time, until she forced him to move to Eden Grove and take care of us. But by then, Theo was a complete delinquent, and I was a cliché of overachievement and loner personality.

Although there *was* a pinprick of light in all that darkness: the piano. One day when I was little, I sat down at Aunt Jeanine's old upright and discovered that I could make sounds. Lines of emotion. *Beauty*.

It was the only joy I had ever experienced in my short, stupid life.

The second or third or fourth time, though, Dad walked in and started screaming at me, tears running down his crazy face. I'm not sure how I managed to play a single note after that. I guess it helps that I'm almost as crazy as he is. It helps, too, that I'm such a master of deception. I practiced in secret all these years and managed to teach myself from YouTube and such.

Dad made noises about selling the piano, but Grandma Min said he couldn't because the house and everything in it belonged to her. He grumbled about it but let it go, I guess, because the piano is still here. Grandma Min is in a nursing home near Tucson now, and she's pretty out of it. Still, whenever we visit her, she squeezes my hand really hard and tells me never to give up.

I'm not sure she knows what she's talking about anymore. But it makes me feel good anyway.

I don't know why I haven't told Plum about all this. Or about how much I wanted—want?—to become a pianist, like Mom. I guess I figured it would never happen, so why bother with a gut-wrenching confession that won't solve anything? *I killed my mom. My dad and brother hate me. I can't become a pianist because I won't hurt my family more than I already have.*

I probably will tell her, someday. That is, if we're still friends, after everything.

As for Dane . . . he actually thinks I *can* become a pianist. Maybe he's crazy too.

Twenty-Three

"Did you see Mr. Rossi while you were in New York City?"

"Actually, he gave me a ride there and back. He wanted to introduce me to Professor van Allstyne personally and also show me around Juilliard."

"I see. And what did the two of you do after your Juilliard appointment?"

"Nothing. He went to visit with some friends, I think. I went to my hotel."

"Which hotel?"

"It was a youth hostel or a Y on West something Street. Or maybe it was East something? I'm sorry, I don't know New York City very well."

"When was the next time you saw Mr. Rossi?"

"That Monday. We met in the Juilliard lobby, and he drove me back home."

"That was it?"

"That was it."

"Have you seen him since then?"

"Sure, in school."

"What about your private lessons? Did they continue?"

"Not really. He helped me with my prescreening recordings, though."

"What is a prescreening recording?"

"I have to play and record a bunch of pieces if I want to apply to Juilliard. Like a classical sonata, a Chopin étude, and so forth. It's a requirement. Same with the other conservatories."

"I see. Miss Kim, at any time did Mr. Rossi say or do anything of a sexual nature while the two of you were in New York City?"

"No. Never."

"How about at school or in his home?"

"No."

"Are you sure?"

"I'm positive."

"Are you in love with Mr. Rossi?"

"Seriously?"

"Please just answer the question."

"No, I'm not in love with Mr. Rossi. Besides, I already have a boyfriend. Braden Hunt."

Twenty-Four

As Dane and I drive across the mile-long George Washington Bridge, everything is shiny and unfamiliar. To the south, the New York City skyline juts across the blue horizon. I spot the silvery point of the Empire State Building, which I recognize from photos and also the movie *King Kong*. Below us, white sailboats dot the Hudson River, which is so wide that it might as well be the ocean.

It's so weird. I was born here. Not that I would remember that time, but still . . .

Dane adjusts his shades, which are very James Bond, and turns up the volume on his car stereo. We have been listening to his favorite opera singer, Jessye Norman, since several toll-booths ago.

"Notice the way she breathes," he tells me. "You'd expect her to take a breath *here*. But no, she takes a breath"—he hums four long beats—"*there*! Isn't it remarkable?"

"Obviously, she has superbreath," I say.

"Superbreath?"

"You know, like Superman? He could hold his breath for a really long time. He could blow out large fires, too. Oh, and once, he saved a town from destruction by inhaling a tornado. He flew up into space and exhaled it out!"

Dane laughs. "I didn't know you were a comic aficionado. I've always been partial to Batman myself."

"Batman, why?"

"I'm not sure. He's dark and mysterious. And he doesn't need superpowers to defeat his evil counterparts."

"True. *And* he's an orphan. Of course, Superman is too, and so is Spider-Man."

"Are you saying that being an orphan is a deficit or an asset?" he asks.

"Both. It sucks not to have parents. On the other hand, if they aren't around, it forces you to be . . . it allows you to be . . ." I search for words. "All three of them, they rose to the occasion."

"Yes, they most certainly did."

We fall silent as the next track begins. The song is "Les Chemins de L'Amour," which I heard once on the radio. I Googled the title; it means "The Paths of Love." Norman's voice is so magnificent, it's like she's singing from her own inner Fortress of Solitude.

I try to ignore the fact that Dane and I are listening to this incredibly romantic song together. And that we are on a road trip to New York City. And that he is wearing his dreamy gray cashmere sweater, the one he wore at Café Tintoretto.

Still, being in my little Dane bubble, my pretending-we're-pianists-together bubble, is so much nicer than dwelling on the rest of my sorry existence.

Jessye Norman finishes with a gorgeous, lingering high note. Dane points to one of the speakers. "Listen! Poulenc wrote that last note as a D-flat. But she goes above and beyond—"

"—and hits the A-flat. Yeah, she's definitely got superpowers."

"You have perfect pitch?" he says, surprised.

"Perfect-*ish*. It's still a work in progress."

"At conservatory you will . . . never mind, here is our exit."

He gets off the bridge and turns onto a road called the West Side Highway. Was he about to tell me more about my imaginary future as a piano performance major? The Hudson River continues to the right of us. To the left are high-rises, a park, and billboards advertising vodka and Broadway shows. I practice arpeggios on my lap, and my fingers make ripples in the green silk of my dress. Dane drives with one hand and conducts Jessye Norman with the other.

We have been on the road since this morning. Dad took off for his office after breakfast, so it was easy to have Dane meet me in front of my house. If Dad had been home, he would have wondered why a strange man in a fancy sports car was picking me up, and not Plum in her parents' Prius. I don't know what would bother Dad more: the fact that I'm visiting Juilliard or the fact that my teacher is driving me there and back. My young, attractive *guy* teacher. But of course Dad is clueless about everything, so it doesn't really matter. In any case, he thinks I'm in Boston for the weekend with Plum, so that's that.

As for Plum, she's under the impression that I'm still in Eden Grove. All week I went back and forth about just telling her the truth. But I couldn't do it. She left for Boston by herself yesterday. She promised to give me full reports on all the schools, and she's already texted me about a million photos of Harvard, Cambridge, and her aunt Jessika's four cats.

She keeps asking me how Theo is.

At some point I am going to have to sort all this out. But I'm not going to think about that now. Juilliard first, difficult conversations later.

Dane turns right at the Seventy-Ninth Street exit, drives

around a traffic circle, and stops at a light. "How are you holding up? Are you tired?"

"I'm fine. Nervous, though."

"Don't be. *Si brillare*."

"What does that mean?"

He turns and smiles at me. "You will shine," he translates.

I will shine.

And then I picture my mother at Juilliard. *She* was the star, the one who was supposed to shine—not me.

"Beatrice, what's wrong?" Dane is staring at me with a worried expression.

"Nothing's wrong. I'm fine."

"We're almost there. Are you ready?"

"Yes. No. Maybe."

He reaches over and squeezes my hand. His touch is warm and strong and reassuring.

I squeeze back. We hold hands for a minute, or maybe many minutes, before he has to let go to shift gears.

Sometimes I'm sorry that he and I ever met, because it's made my life so much more confusing.

But right now is not one of those times.

TWENTY-FIVE

We have arrived at Juilliard.

It is smaller than I expected and also more spectacular. The main entrance is all glass with THE JUILLIARD SCHOOL spelled out in silver letters. On the other side of the glass is a massive staircase that ascends up, up, up to some mysterious apex.

Being here, I am filled with sadness and wonder. *This was her place.* I don't know a lot about her years here—just what Grandma Min told me a long time ago. She said that Mom and Dad started dating when she was a freshman and he was finishing up at Columbia Law School. She said it was love at first sight, at least for Dad, who couldn't stop talking about her to the family.

She also said I should stop feeling guilty about her death, but I can't seem to do that.

Dane and I stand on the sidewalk as students come and go through the revolving door, chattering easily:

"It's for three-handed piano and four soloists."

"Three-handed piano?"

"Two pianists on one piano, but the one closest to the audience has only a single line."

"Hey, who's applying to Verbier next summer?"

"Dude, no one gets into that."

"Jonathan did last year."

"Yeah, well, JONATHAN."

"Anyone go to the master class yesterday?"

"Uh-huh. Tabitha got spanked."

"Why did she pick 'Caténaires'? Her contemporary technique sucks. . . ."

An icy ball of terror has begun to form in my stomach. "I can't do this," I whisper to Dane.

"Yes, you can."

"I don't belong here."

"Nonsense, of course you do. Come on, let's go inside."

He puts his hand on the small of my back and gently nudges me through the revolving door. A gust of air stirs my hair and rustles my dress. As we start up the staircase, we pass more students—talking, texting, cradling instrument cases between their legs. I overhear bits and pieces of conversation—"Banff," "vocal collab," "circle of fifths,"

"Horizons requirement"—and it is all a foreign language to me.

Did Mom speak this language too? How did she manage to fit in?

The top of the staircase opens up to a vast, starkly beautiful lobby. Security guards preside at a long desk. Several professor types confer with a man who is the spitting image of Yo-Yo Ma.

Wait, it *is* Yo-Yo Ma.

The beyond-famous cellist and Dane wave at each other.

"You *know* him?" I gasp.

"I've met him on several occasions. Very nice man. He's playing with the Phil, I believe this evening."

"You mean the New York Philharmonic? The orchestra?"

"Yes, exactly."

Dane gives our names to one of the guards, who glances at a clipboard and admits us through the turnstile. A few minutes later we are on the fourth floor in search of a practice room so I can warm up.

As we proceed down the hall, music pours out from behind closed doors: "Vissi d'arte" sung by a pitch-perfect soprano; the cadenza from the Sibelius violin concerto; an impossible passage from the piano transcription of Stravinsky's *Petrushka*. The icy ball of terror grows larger. I am so out of my league here, it's not even funny.

"Beatrice." Dane squeezes my shoulder. "It will be fine. *You'll* be fine."

"But everyone here is so crazy talented."

"Yes, and so are you. Never forget that."

We find an empty practice room at the end of the hall. Inside is a Steinway baby grand with a faded mahogany finish. I wonder if Mom ever practiced in this room, at this very piano. On the floor is an empty Pinkberry container, a *People* magazine, and a chewed-up No. 2 pencil.

Dane leans over the keyboard and plays a B-flat scale. "Well, it's *almost* in tune. Go ahead, you try it."

He steps aside to make room for me. I sit down, adjust my skirt, and play a B-flat scale too. I follow this with some Hanon exercises. My fingers feel cold and stiff. I stop playing and rub my hands together.

Dane reaches into his messenger bag and retrieves his leather gloves. "Here, put these on for a few minutes."

"Thanks." I slip them on and hold them up. "I look ridiculous!"

"You look adorable. Do you know what I used to do before performances?"

Adorable?

"Most musicians have pre-performance rituals to help calm their nerves," he goes on. "I used to do maths in my head. Eight times seventeen, nine hundred minus thirty-six, and so on. It gets you out of the panic part of your brain and into a more rational part. One of my friends, who was also a pianist, would play video games for an hour. His favorite was Plants vs. Zombies. Another friend liked to jump rope backstage."

"No way. Really?"

"You'll develop your own rituals, I'm sure. Taking a walk, repeating a mantra, eating a particular snack. Wearing lucky socks. We musicians are quite a superstitious bunch."

"My mom—," I begin.

His expression softens. "Yes? What about your mother?"

"Nothing. It's not important. I'm going to practice the Ocean Etude now."

I pull off his gloves and set them down on the bench beside me, one on top of the other. My hands aren't totally warmed up, but I need to play. And to stop talking.

As I plunge into the familiar piece, the icy ball starts to thaw and dissipate. The arpeggios rise and fall, one wave after another, tumbling over each other and yet producing a single line of sound. Soon the C-minor key resolves to C major, and agitation becomes triumph . . . sweetness . . . light.

I wanted to tell him. There is so much I want to tell

him. The small stuff, the big stuff, even the bottomless-pit-of-despair stuff. He understands me; he understands about music.

But first I need to get through the next few hours. Rise to the occasion, even. Strangely, I'm beginning to think that this day actually might matter, one way or the other.

TWENTY-SIX

Annaliese van Allstyne kisses Dane on both cheeks.

"It has been much too long, Gabriel," she chides him affectionately.

Why "Gabriel"?

Her accent is exotic and unfamiliar, some combination of French and German and other languages I've probably never heard of. I vaguely recall hearing that she grew up in Switzerland or maybe South Africa. We are in her fifth-floor studio, which has not one but *two* grand pianos—a Steinway and something called a Fazioli.

"*Je suis désolé. Mon nouvel emploi—,*" Dane replies.

"*Oui, oui.* We must have a talk about your career later."

"Of course." He gestures for me to come forward. "Beatrice, I'd like you to meet Annaliese van Allstyne. Annaliese, this is Beatrice Kim."

Annaliese extends her hand. *"Enchanté.* It is a pleasure to meet you, my dear."

She looks exactly as she does on her CD covers and website and press photos: petite frame, piercing blue eyes, and whitish-blond hair tied back in an elegant knot. Her only accessory is a simple diamond brooch that glitters against her gray wool dress.

This is Annaliese van Allstyne, I think, and I am so awestruck that I can barely speak.

Dane clears his throat and touches my elbow.

"T-thank you so much for seeing me, P-professor van Allstyne," I stammer as I shake her small, delicate hand. I've heard her perform Tchaikovsky's Piano Concerto No. 1; how does she manage all those insane octaves with such a limited reach?

"Please, call me Annaliese. 'Professor' sounds so old, and I am still vain enough to care about that sort of thing. Gabriel has told me a great deal about you. He says you are fond of Schumann."

"Yes, I love Schumann."

"Do you know his *Davidsbündlertänze*? The 'Dances of the League of David'?"

"That's the . . . I have a recording of it with Murray Perahia."

"Ah, yes, he is marvelous! Have you also heard Mitsuko Uchida's recording?"

"I don't think so."

"Well, you must. She has an exquisite sense of the German *innig* marking."

"Innish?" I echo back.

"Yes. *Innig* is a difficult word to explain. It means to perform a piece not just for the audience as a whole, but in a personal, intimate way for each individual. A kind of spiritual connection with the listener, if you will. A tenderness, a sharing of the self." Annaliese smiles serenely and leans against the Fazioli. "So, my dear. I want to know more about you. How long have you been playing the piano?"

"Well, um, a long time. Since I was little."

"Gabriel tells me that you have never had formal training."

"Not really, no."

"Do you come from a musical family? Your father, your mother, siblings?"

I fiddle with my ponytail, tightening it and then wrapping it around my fingers. I guess Dane didn't mention my mom to Annaliese. "Well, um, my brother plays guitar in a band."

Dane raises his eyebrows.

"I see." Her forehead furrows as she points to the Steinway. "Would you like to begin with the Fantasy? Or a different piece?"

"The Fantasy's fine."

"*Très bien*. Gabriel, leave us."

"But, Annaliese—"

She shoots him a stern look. He sighs and turns to me. "I'll be in the hall if you need me."

I nod mutely. The terror is threatening to trickle back. *I can't do this . . .*

"Beatrice."

"Yes?"

Dane leans over and hugs me. I can feel the heat of his palms through the thin silk fabric of my dress. "*Si brillare*," he whispers in my ear.

The door closes behind him. I stand there, a little breathless.

"Shall we?" Annaliese prompts.

"Yes, I'm sorry . . . "

I sit down at the Steinway, adjusting the bench, fussing with my skirt. I try to remember everything Dane taught me about the Fantasy: lose myself, sleepwalk, wander off the map. But all I can think about is the sensation of his arms around me. He has never held me before.

Annaliese takes a seat at the Fazioli, crosses her legs, and slips on a pair of glasses. She probably wants me to start playing already. I need to get a grip here.

I position my thumbs on middle C and run through some scales, in opposite directions, to test the action. It's a little heavy, and the keys resist; I will have to compensate with a quicker attack.

Annaliese watches me intently. "So that is how you hold your wrists?"

She hates the way I hold my wrists. "Y-yes."

"Interesting. Please, proceed."

Really, I'm supposed to play after *that*? With that one politely dismissive comment, I can feel my entire musical infrastructure collapsing. My wrists are wrong . . . that must mean my fingers are wrong too . . . not to mention my fingering, my phrasing, my breathing. Everything I've done has become undone. There is no way I can perform the Fantasy now, or "Old MacDonald," or anything.

I am two seconds away from a full-blown panic attack when her voice comes to me. *Her* voice, or at least how I always imagined it.

I'm right here with you.

I am not aware of when I start to play. Something possesses me, and I fall, collapse into the opening notes. It's like I'm watching myself in a dream, except it's not really me. I'm not here; I'm someone else; I'm completely free of my body.

Soon my left hand becomes a constant current; my right hand becomes a passionate plea. Then the music shifts into quiet sweetness. It shifts again, exploding into desolate octaves.

Minutes pass like seconds. I am so connected to the piece that I don't even hear myself. The first movement flows into the second movement, which flows into the third.

When the last chords fade away, I awaken from the spell. My cheeks are wet with tears.

I sit up straight and swipe at them with my sleeve. What happened? Was my performance a disaster? I can barely make myself look at Annaliese.

I feel her hand on my shoulder.

"Oh, my dear girl," is all she says.

I glance up in surprise. She is crying too.

TWENTY-SEVEN

"She said I reminded her of a young Martha Argerich. And that my technique is quite extraordinary—those were her exact words, 'quite extraordinary.' I thought she didn't like my wrists at first. But then it turned out she *did* like them; she just wasn't expecting someone my age, with my background, to know how to position them properly. She wants me to check out this one Chopin étude to help me with my reach—she says it's all about rolling through thirteenths, can you believe it? *Thirteenths!* She also wants me to learn a concerto. She suggested Brahms One—is that the one in D minor?—or maybe the Grieg. Have you ever played the Grieg? Oh, and I almost forgot, she said that my Beethoven was 'spot-on' . . . that's a good thing, right, 'spot-on'? . . . and . . ."

I can't stop talking, I am so keyed up. It's like I've had ten espressos. Dane walks beside me, his hands clasped behind his back, just listening. It is Saturday night, balmy for October, and the Juilliard neighborhood is bustling.

I am babbling on about Annaliese's views on Ravel versus Debussy when I realize that he is laughing at me. I stop in my tracks, causing a minor traffic jam on the sidewalk.

"What is so funny?" I demand.

"Not funny. Delightful. I've never seen you so elated. One would think you'd won the lottery."

"Well, of course I'm happy! I mean, *Annaliese van Allstyne*. She's . . . she's . . . I can't believe she liked me! Liked my playing! I was sure she was going to throw me out of her studio, you know, all 'Please don't waste my time with your amateurish regurgitations.'"

"Amateurish regurgitations? Really, Beatrice."

"How long have you known her? How did you end up with her as a teacher? Has she always been this awesome? Why does she call you 'Gabriel'? Tell me everything!"

"Yes. But first let's get some dinner. I'm famished—aren't you famished?"

"I'm too excited to eat!"

"Nevertheless. And she calls me 'Gabriel' because I didn't start going by 'Dane' until after college."

"Really?"

"Really."

He leads me around the corner to a little French restaurant. There seems to be thousands of restaurants in New York City. The maître d' guy directs us to one of the outdoor tables, next to a glowing patio heater, and hands us a couple of menus. I touch a pink rosebud that sits in a vase next to a flickering white candle. When the waiter comes by, Dane rattles off a bunch of stuff to him in French.

"Excuse me, what?" I ask as I try to decipher the menu.

"I ordered us some appetizers. For the main course I recommend the *poulet rôti* or the *cassoulet*. *Poulet rôti* is roast chicken, and *cassoulet* is . . . well, it's this very nice sort of casserole from the south of France."

"I guess you've been here before, then?"

"Actually, Annaliese brought me here to celebrate after my graduation. So I thought it would be appropriate to bring you here tonight."

"Oh!" I flush with pleasure. "That's so . . . wow, thank you!"

"You're welcome."

After a few minutes the waiter brings us our *entrées:* raw oysters, scallops cooked in cream and cheese, and a little pot of chicken liver pâté with bread. I've had fancy food before, mostly at the Sorensons', but not *this* fancy. I stare at the dishes, not knowing what I'm supposed to do with them exactly. Do I eat the oysters with a fork? Do I dip the bread in the pâté?

The waiter also brings us a bottle of champagne with two glasses. He pours a small amount for Dane, who tastes it, nods, and says something in French.

After the waiter leaves, Dane turns to me. "I'm sorry. I'm not sure why he brought two glasses. I ordered you some sparkling water; he's bringing it now."

"What kind is champagne is it? The bottle's really pretty."

"It's from a vineyard in Ambonnay, which is a small town in northeastern France. My grandparents, my mother's parents, had a house there; my grandmother was French. It's where we used to spend many of our summer holidays."

"Can I have a tiny little sip?"

"Um . . . all right, yes. Just a tiny little sip."

He pours me half a glass, and the bubbles make a quiet, pleasant hissing sound. I raise the glass to my lips. The bubbles tickle.

"It tastes like very expensive grapes," I remark.

"Yes it does, doesn't it? My father let me have my first glass of champagne when I was eleven. I remember thinking that it was perfectly dreadful."

I smile. "When did you decide it was good?"

"My sixteenth birthday. I stole a couple of bottles from my parents' cellar so I could get blotto with my mates."

"Did you get caught?"

"Unfortunately, yes. My mum and dad kept very close tabs on me."

I take a bite of the cheesy scallops and wash it down with more champagne. I can't believe I'm in New York City, having dinner with Dane in a French restaurant. "What was it like, growing up with famous musician parents and a famous musician sister? Is that why you decided to study piano?" I ask him.

A strange expression clouds Dane's face. "How did you—"

Stupid, stupid. He doesn't know that I looked him up.

"I'm sorry . . . I didn't mean to . . ." I set my fork and glass down, embarrassed. "I, um, Googled you. I was trying to find Annaliese's name, back before you told me what it was. I happened to see this other stuff about you and your family and . . . I'm really sorry . . . Did I screw up? I screwed up, didn't I?"

"It's fine, I understand." He looks preoccupied as he pours more champagne into his glass. "My parents wanted my sister and me to become professional musicians, just like them. They started Lisette on voice lessons at an early age. With me, it was piano. I wanted to please them, so I worked hard and took to it quickly. They, along with my teacher at the time, Rafael Silva, entered me in all sorts of competitions and arranged recitals for me at all sorts of important venues. By the time I was a teenager, they had me on a fast track to becoming a concert pianist. Then, after grade eleven, I was accepted to Juilliard, and

Annaliese became my teacher. She had just joined the faculty. After I graduated, though . . ." His voice trails off.

"What?"

"I moved back to London. I concertized a bit. I took on a few students. But I wasn't happy."

"Why not?"

Dane shrugs. "I wasn't sure I *wanted* to be a professional musician. So eventually, I stopped concertizing. I traveled; I lived in Paris for a while; then I returned to the States. I taught music at a prep school. But that wasn't right for me either. I was a bit lost, to tell you the truth."

"But how did you end up at A- . . . at Andrew Jackson?"

"It was a favor for an old classmate. She called me and said she wanted to take some extra months off for her maternity leave. But the school, your school, was having a hard time finding a replacement. She asked if I knew anyone, and I thought, why not me? I didn't have anything else going on, and I thought the change of scene might do me good."

"Wait, *what*? Mrs. Singh is your *friend*? And she went to *Juilliard*?"

"Yes. She plays the viola, didn't you know?" Dane downs his champagne. "But enough about me. Let's talk about you."

I really, really want to ask him more personal questions. Like how his superstar parents feel about his being a sub at a middle-of-nowhere American high school. Or what he plans to do with the rest of his life. He's such an incredible pianist; I can't imagine him *not* being a professional musician.

Also, what did he mean, *lost*? I thought only people like me felt that way.

But I guess he's done sharing for the night. "What do you want to know about me? My favorite color? Blue. My favorite dessert? Coffee ice cream with a big, huge swirl of whipped cream on top. My favorite composer? I have, like, six—no, seven—of them."

Dane laughs. "Actually, I want to know what you think of Juilliard."

"Are you serious? I loved it!"

"You're probably wondering what happens next, then."

"With what?"

"With Annaliese. She and I spoke briefly after your meeting. She told me that she would be happy to have you as a student."

"Is that a good thing?"

"It's a fantastic thing. She only accepts one or two new people into her studio every year, if that."

I let this sink in for a moment. "Wow. Okay. So, how does that work?"

"Well, to begin with, you will have to apply to Juilliard for next fall. That means filling out a lot of paperwork, making a prescreening recording, and so forth. I can help you with the recording. If you pass that stage, you will be asked to appear for a live audition, in March, I believe."

"A live audition? That sounds completely terrifying."

"Yes and no. The entire piano faculty will be there, including Annaliese. Afterward, she will indicate on a form that she would be willing to have you as a student in her studio. Some or all of the other piano faculty may do the same. Other things will happen that day—an interview, sight-reading, et cetera. Then your file goes to the admissions committee, and the final decision is up to them."

"Okay. Wow."

"If you wish to apply to other conservatories as well, I would suggest New England Conservatory, Curtis, Peabody, Manhattan School of Music. Possibly some other schools. I can recommend teachers at each of them. I'm happy to take you for visits too." Dane adds, "Ultimately, you should pick your school based on whom you wish to study with. So if you want to study with Annaliese, you should aim for Juilliard. Do you want to study with Annaliese?"

"Definitely, yes. Except . . . "

"Except what?"

I pick up my champagne glass. It's empty. "Can we change

the subject? I really just want to enjoy dinner and gab about random stuff, like movies or Mr. Yo-Yo Ma or why that woman over there is wearing a dead fox on her head. And maybe later, after I'm nice and drunk, I'll tell you *my* life story."

"You are not going to get nice and drunk. I'm cutting you off."

But when I reach for the bottle, he doesn't stop me.

He's definitely not acting like a teacher anymore.

The waiter clears our plates and gives us more plates. The food looks amazing, but I'm not sure I can keep eating. There's so much to process: Juilliard, prescreening recordings, live auditions. It's like my very own version of Plum's Golden Notebook.

But am I deluding myself? I'm deluding myself. Even if I *could* get into Juilliard, there's no way I can go. Dad really *would* have a stroke, and Theo . . . well, he'd probably never speak to me again. Or he'd punch me in the face. Or all of the above.

The sky is a dark, velvety blue. An autumn chill has descended on the evening. The woman with the fox hat holds hands with a guy who looks way too young to be her husband or boyfriend.

I tip back my champagne. "Is there an ocean near here?" I ask Dane.

"Yes, of course there's an ocean near here. We're on the East Coast. That's the Atlantic." He nods in some vague direction.

"Can we go? Please?"

"Can we go . . . to the ocean?"

"Yes. I've never been."

"But we have a long drive ahead of us."

"I know. But can't we stop at a beach on the way?"

"I suppose so."

Apparently, I have decided to wander off the map.

Apparently, so has he.

TWENTY-EIGHT

After dinner Dane drives us to a place called Whiterock Beach. I'm not sure how long the drive takes—maybe an hour, maybe more. I am too busy admiring the scenery through my giddy champagne haze: the glittery lights, the neon signs, the grid of buildings packed one against the other across forever. At some point we drive over a bridge, and the landscape loosens, becomes more suburban.

When we get to our destination, Dane parks the car on a street lined with colorful row houses. "It was a toss-up between Long Beach, Brighton Beach, Far Rockaway, and here," he explains. "This place was always my favorite. My Juilliard mates and I used to come out here on weekends when we needed to get away."

"Get away from what?"

"Practicing. The pressure. There's something about the

ocean that makes your problems seem very small and trivial."

"Like nature's Valium?"

He grins. "Yes, like nature's Valium."

We leave the car and follow a sandy, grassy path. The air is cool and salty and intoxicating. My shoes—my one good pair of shoes, with the black patent leather and sensible heels—sink softly as I walk. As we near the beach, I can hear the waves rolling in.

"Watch your step," Dane says, holding my elbow.

We seem to be the only people around. "Are we allowed to be here?"

"Yes, it's fine. It's a public beach."

We climb a small embankment, and as we come down the other side, *there it is.* The ocean—finally, at last. It is endless and dark, stretching from here to beyond. The waves lap against the shore with a steady, then not-steady rhythm that is at once jarring and hypnotic.

"I can't believe I'm here," I whisper.

"I gather you like the ocean?"

"Not just *like.* This has been my . . . I've wanted to see the ocean, any ocean, ever since I can remember."

"So your family didn't go on beach holidays?"

"My family didn't, doesn't, go on *any* holidays. Except to fly out to Arizona to visit my grandma once in a while."

He doesn't say anything. Instead, he drapes his arm around my shoulder, and we walk toward the water together.

"Can I take off my shoes?" I ask.

"Yes, you can take off your shoes."

"Turn around."

"What?"

"Turn around. Please."

He does so, and I quickly remove my heels and panty hose. Then I hoist up the hem of my dress and run into the waves.

The hit of cold makes me shriek and giggle simultaneously.

"Are you all right?" Dane calls out.

"Yes, I'm great! You should come in!"

He hesitates for a moment before taking off his own shoes and socks and rolling up his pants. He steps tentatively into the water and makes a face.

"How on earth can you stand this temperature?"

"Wow, you are such a wuss."

He kicks water at me. I kick water back at him.

"All right, stop that now. I'm completely drenched," he orders me.

"You started it!"

We stop splashing and catch our breath. A tiny boat appears out of nowhere and drifts slowly across the horizon, its red sidelight blinking on and off.

Then fast-forward . . . and Dane and I are standing side by side, our hands brushing lightly against each other. How did that happen? Is ocean-time different, less linear? Or maybe everything seems less linear after drinking champagne.

I swoon a little, and he grabs my wrist.

"Are you all right?"

"Yes. Are you?"

"Yes. Beatrice, can I ask you something?"

"Hmm."

"Has your father forbidden you to go to Juilliard? Because it's where your mother went?"

"Um . . ." I drop my gaze. In the moonlight I can see the faint traces of the last pedi Plum gave me, which alternates pink, purple, pink, purple. I wonder what she's doing right now? She hasn't texted me in a while. Also, I think my phone battery may have died.

"I understand that the memories may be painful for him. Losing someone you love . . . it's . . . Still, I would think he would be proud that you're a pianist, that you're carrying on her tradition," Dane continues.

Maybe I should have gone to Boston with Plum after all. Fake-smiling my way through all those college tours, acting like I really wanted to be there . . .

"Also, and not to be insensitive to your father's feelings,

but . . . you *are* an adult, or you will be soon. You should be able to choose your profession and what college you go to. And if you're concerned that he won't pay for a conservatory education for you, well, there are scholarships we can look into—"

"Mismatched earrings," I cut in.

"Excuse me?"

"Mismatched earrings. Like, one silver and one gold. Or one heart and one moon. That was my mom's pre-performance ritual. She thought it was good luck to wear them. That's what my grandma told me, anyway."

Dane's gaze shift to my ears. He reaches out and touches the right ear, then the left. "One diamond and one emerald," he notes.

His cool fingers on my earlobes make me dizzy with pleasure. I want him to keep touching me like that. "One *faux* diamond and one *faux* emerald. See, I know French," I murmur.

"I can't tell that they're fake. You look beautiful in them."

"Oh!"

His hand drops to my cheek and caresses it. "Beatrice, I want so much to help you. *Please* let me help you."

He is so earnest and caring and kind. I don't know what to say. Besides Grandma Min, he is the only one who has ever encouraged me to pursue my dream.

Also, I think I'm falling for him.

Overcome with emotion, I lean my head against his chest. His cashmere sweater is as soft as I imagined it would be, and I want to lose myself in it.

In response Dane wraps his arms around me and holds me close. It feels . . . *perfect*. Meant to be. We stand like this for a long time, listening to the ocean.

And then I tip my head up, and his lips are right there, first pressing against my hair, then my forehead, then my eyelids, then my lips. He kisses me . . . I kiss him back . . . we are kissing. *Oh my God, we are kissing.* We are tentative at first, and then more urgent, as though we have to fit everything, all of this, into a few precious seconds.

His mouth tastes warm and sweet and slightly salty. His body envelops mine as his hands find the low curve of my back and pull me closer . . . closer.

He pushes away abruptly. "We can't."

"Why?"

"Because you're . . . Listen, love, this can't happen."

"Why?"

"Because I could get into a lot of trouble. Come on, I'm taking you home."

But he doesn't move, and neither do I. I reach out and trail my fingers down his arm. I have no idea what I'm doing or where this is going, but it really doesn't matter. When his lips find mine again, I surrender completely.

"We should—," he whispers.

"Yes," I whisper back.

He takes my hand and leads me to his car.

TWENTY-NINE

We go to the Whiterock Motel, which is down the street from the beach. I wait in the car while Dane registers us at the front office.

While he's gone, I fluff my hair in the rearview mirror. My eyes are bright, and my cheeks are flushed. I can't believe this is happening. I've thought about him and wanted him for so long, and now, finally . . .

He slides into the driver's seat and hands me a plastic card.

"What's this?" I ask.

"It's the key to your room. It's next to mine."

"Two rooms? But I thought—"

"I know, but . . . you need your sleep."

"I don't want to sleep."

"Neither do I. But it's best this way. Come on, I'll show you to your room."

"But, Dane!"

"Please, Beatrice. We can talk about this in the morning."

Confused, I scoop up my backpack, which contains my sheet music, wallet, and a few other random items. My only clothes are the outfit I'm wearing and my jacket. Dane is already out of the car, hands stuffed in pockets, striding across the nearly empty parking lot with his messenger bag.

I catch up to him, and we walk in silence to the end of the one-story building that has palm trees painted on it. A sliver of ocean gleams dully in the distance. Across the street are a forlorn-looking diner and a drugstore, both with OPEN signs.

I follow Dane to a turquoise door marked 18. He stands aside as I insert the plastic card in a slit above the doorknob. Nothing happens.

"Here, allow me." Dane takes the card from me and inserts it. The door makes a *click,* and he pushes it open.

He waves me inside but remains stoically in the doorway. "I'll see you in the morning. We can have breakfast at that diner over there before we head for home. Make sure you call or text your father and let him know you've been . . . delayed."

Dane doesn't know that Dad thinks I'm in Boston until Monday.

"Fine," I mumble.

"Good night, then."

"Good night."

He hesitates, then cradles my face with his hand. For a second I think he's going to kiss me, and my heart thrums in my chest.

Then he turns abruptly and heads for his room.

I hear his door shut and lock.

Wrong again.

Stifling my disappointment, I flick on the light switch and survey my room. The décor is 1970s furniture, flamingo wallpaper, and a huge orange bed.

The sight of the bed makes my cheeks hot. I try not to imagine Dane and me lying on top of it, our bodies entwined...

Stop it.

I wander over to the adjoining bathroom, which is the size of a closet. Tiny soaps, shampoos, and lotions line the sink. And then I realize: I didn't bring any toiletries with me. I hadn't expected to stay overnight. I can live without most of the stuff, but I absolutely need a few basic items like contact lens solution.

Sighing, I grab my key card and wallet and head back outside.

This night is turning out to be one big anticlimax.

• • •

Back from the drugstore I take out my contacts, brush my teeth, and get ready for bed. Since I didn't bring pj's, I strip down to my underwear, which totally don't match: a pink lace bra and leopard panties—some combination.

For a while I skim through *Love in the Time of Cholera*, which I've already read twice by now. The first time through, I tried to imagine that I was Fermina Daza and Dane was her forbidden lover, Florentino Ariza. The second time, I switched it around so that Dane was Fermina's husband, Juvenal Urbino, instead.

Now I'm rereading the scene where Fermina loses her virginity to Juvenal during their honeymoon. I get through a couple of sentences until I can't stand it anymore. I bury the book under my pillow and switch on the TV.

The local news. A hockey game. A *Friends* rerun. Nothing interesting.

Finally, I give up and turn off the TV and lights and just lie there. The air smells like the motel moisturizer on my hands, all vanilla and lime and mint. Specks of beach sand grind between my toes.

The clock blinks at me: 1:05 a.m. Gossamer moon shadows flit across the ceiling. I picture them dancing to the wispy, watery notes of Ravel's "Une barque sur l'ocean." When that's finished, I make them dance to Debussy's "En Bateau."

I wonder if Dane likes those pieces.

I wonder if he is still awake too.

I wonder where he learned to kiss like that. Like the way he plays Bach's Goldberg Variations, so softly and passionately and . . .

The next thing I know, I'm getting up and putting on my dress and jacket. Five minutes later I am at his door.

Don't knock, I tell myself.

I knock.

Dane opens the door. He is wearing only jeans. I stare at his bare chest and gulp.

"Beatrice, what's wrong?"

"I can't sleep."

He rakes his hand through his hair. "You're not wearing shoes. Why can't you sleep?"

"Because."

"Go back to your room, love."

"No."

"Listen to me, this is a very bad idea—"

Before he can say anything more, I wrap my arms around his neck and kiss him.

He jerks back, breathing heavily. "Beatrice . . . "

"Please, Dane, I really want to."

I kiss him again, and this time he doesn't resist. He slips his hands under my jacket and caresses my back, pulls me closer. We stumble across the threshold, still kissing as he kicks the door shut.

Yes yes yes.

I shrug out of my jacket as we tumble onto the bed. The bright orange quilt is smooth and intact, and a Stravinsky score lies on top of it, open. I realize with a start that he's been wide awake all this time too.

He swats the score aside. And then he is on top of me, kissing me everywhere . . . my lips, my face, my neck.

"We shouldn't be doing this," he murmurs into my hair.

"I know."

"Are you sure it's okay?"

"Yes, it's more than okay."

He helps me out of my dress. I reach behind and unhook my bra. He leans down and kisses my breasts, tenderly at first, then not so tenderly. I give a little cry.

"Sorry! Did I—"

"No, do that again. Please."

He kisses my breasts some more. The pleasure is so intense, I can barely stand it.

I can feel him straining against his jeans. I fumble around for his zipper.

"Beatrice, I don't . . . that is, I don't have—"

"That's okay. I do."

He pulls back and blinks at me in surprise. "You brought condoms?"

"No. I bought some at the drugstore across the street. They're in my jacket pocket."

"Crazy girl."

"I know. Please, do that thing again."

He obliges. Pale moonlight spills into the room as he teases and torments me with his mouth. *God*, it was so not like this with Braden . . . or Andy McDermott . . . or Gil Northman . . . or anyone else in the universe, past, present, or future.

After I can't take it anymore, he stands up and steps out of his jeans and his boxers, his eyes never leaving mine.

Dane, naked. There are no words.

"Are you sure this is what you want?" he asks me hoarsely.

"Yes. Oh my God, yes."

As I slip off my panties, he gets a condom from my jacket and returns to the bed. A moment later he arcs over me.

"Can I—"

"Yes!"

I arch my body to meet his and bury my face in his neck.

Yes yes yes yes yes.

THIRTY

Morning. My eyelids flutter against bright sunlight. It takes me a minute to realize that I am not in my bed at home. I am in *this* bed, in a motel, with Dane.

Dane.

His eyes are closed, and his chest rises and falls silently. I curl against him and breathe in the smell of his skin, which is salt and cologne, sweat and us. The last twenty-four hours— were they a dream? They were not a dream. Juilliard, Annaliese, the French restaurant, the beach . . . and what we did all night afterward.

The rest of the world seems very far away, and I'm not sure I want to go back.

"Beatrice?"

Dane stirs and rolls over. I reach out and touch his stubbly face. Even first thing in the morning on almost no sleep, he is ridiculously good-looking.

He takes my hand and kisses it lightly. "How are you?"

"I'm fine. Last night, was I . . . did I . . . ?" I stumble around for the right words. "I've never done that before," I confess.

"I'm your first?" Dane says incredulously.

I nod.

He strokes my hair. "You were perfect. You *are* perfect."

"Really?"

"Really."

"I thought the first time was supposed to be awkward and awful, but . . ." I blush. "It wasn't."

"No, it wasn't."

He draws me closer to him and kisses my head. "Listen, love," he says, and his voice sounds different: distracted, pensive. "Last night was wonderful. But when we get back to Eden Grove, we . . . we can't continue."

"What?" I pull back and stare at him. "Why not?"

"Because I'm . . . we just *can't*. You know that. You're my student, and I'm your teacher. Not to mention the fact that I'm twenty-seven years old, and you're still a minor."

The real world is creeping back.

"No one has to know," I point out.

"Someone at school is bound to find out."

"We could just meet at your house and never see each other at the school. I'll drop out of your class, switch to another elective. You could stop coaching Braden and Lianna and me."

"What about your friend?"

Plum. I cringe as I remember all the lies I've fed her.

"Plum used to tease me that I had a big crush on you. But she doesn't know . . . I mean, I didn't tell her . . . In any case, she thinks I'm home with my dad and brother this weekend."

"What about your father? Won't he mention your New York trip to her? Then she might figure it out."

"Yeah, well . . . my dad thinks I'm in Boston with Plum."

Dane's eyes widen. "You didn't tell your father you were going to New York instead?"

"No."

"Is that wise? I know he's not supportive of your playing the piano, but . . . "

"Seriously, he has no idea where I am half the time. He's constantly working."

"Still, at some point you *will* have to talk to him about everything. Juilliard, your music."

"I know, I know."

We lapse into an uneasy silence. Dane turns away from me and gazes out the window. Our view, if you can call it that, is of a wooden fence. A skinny yellow cat perches precariously on top of it, which makes me think of Cream Puff.

Dane swings his legs over the side of the bed, reaches for his jeans, and tugs them on. When he gets up and walks over to the window, his shoulders are tense.

He presses his palm against the glass, and it leaves a print. He quickly wipes it away.

"Listen. I want to tell you something," he says in a quiet voice.

I frown. Is this going to be one of those talks? *I have a girlfriend. I'm married. I'm moving back to London.* The real world is returning with a vengeance. I sit up straight, bunch the sheet around me, and brace myself for what's coming.

"In the beginning I thought I was just killing time at Andrew Jackson. Helping a friend. And then I met you—" He stops.

I let go of my death grip on the sheets. Maybe it's not bad news after all.

"Working with you, teaching you, coaching you . . . I've loved every second, and not just because of how I feel about . . . Anyway, it's made me think about going back to school myself. Graduate school, that is," he goes on.

Graduate school? Relieved, I slump back against the pillows.

"With a master's and a doctorate, I would be qualified to

teach plus coach at the college level. I'm thinking that might be a good path for me."

"You told me last night that your parents wanted you to become a concert pianist. Have you given up on that?"

"That was their dream, not mine. I love music, and I love the piano. But the stage is not for me."

"Oh."

"You, on the other hand . . . I predict you'll become one of the greatest concert pianists of your generation."

"I don't think so," I say, flattered. Except . . . *my* generation? Why not *our* generation?

"Anyway, my job at Andrew Jackson will likely end after Christmas. Elena thinks she'll be ready to return then. In the meantime, I can start filling out graduate school applications for next fall."

What about us? I want to ask. "Wow. I'm really happy for you," I say, plucking at the sheet.

"I'm not finished. I'll probably be applying to a number of master's programs, including the ones at Juilliard and the Manhattan School of Music. If you decide to apply to those schools too, maybe we'll both end up in New York. And then we could try this for real. That is, if you want to."

He sounds shy and nervous, like the first time he asked me to play the Schumann for him.

My heart races wildly.

Dane and me in New York City together.

All of a sudden, the thought of discussing my future with Dad doesn't seem quite as scary anymore. Being honest with him, being honest with myself . . . it all seems possible now.

I smile at Dane. "Yes."

"Really? Yes?"

In two seconds he is by my side, kissing and caressing me. The world disappears again.

THIRTY-ONE

It is almost eight o'clock on Monday night when Dane pulls up in front of my house. We're still in our clothes from Saturday, and I can feel sand in my hair and shoes. We had meant to leave the Whiterock Motel yesterday, but we couldn't seem to tear ourselves away. We ordered in from the diner and ate our meals in bed. We went out only to take long walks along the beach; once, we even made love there under the stars.

The moon is high in the sky and casts a pale white glow on our faces as Dane draws me to him and kisses me good night. When we finally pull away, he is smiling, but his smile has a penumbra of sadness.

"Thank you for everything," I say, meaning it.

"This weekend, I . . . " He hesitates. "I'm incredibly proud of what you accomplished in New York with Annaliese."

"Thanks. Thank you. You helped me so much with that."

"And I'm going to continue helping you."

"Thank you. I'll talk to my dad soon, I promise."

"Good girl."

Just then a huge SUV drives toward us, flooding the inside of Dane's car with its high beams. Dane cringes and covers his face with the back of his hand. I instinctively slide down in my seat.

When the car passes, Dane turns to me. "Beatrice?"

"Yes?"

"I meant what I said before. We can't see each other, at least not until you turn eighteen. It's against the law, on top of which, it's against school rules for teachers to date students."

Stupid laws. Stupid rules. "I'll turn eighteen in December," I point out.

"And after Christmas I won't be a teacher at Andrew Jackson anymore. Things will be easier for us then. In the meantime, we have to act purely professional, platonic, whatever the term is. I think it's a good idea, too, what you said about dropping my class. Also, I'll step down from coaching the trio."

"Okay."

We kiss again before I get out of the car. He lingers at the curb until I reach the front door and then drives off. My lips tingle, and my mind hums with happy memories of the last forty-eight hours. I'm already missing that time. How will I manage without it? I know I'm good at lying, but will I be able to pretend to other people that he's just my teacher?

Light seeps from inside the house. I can hear voices.

Puzzled, I press my ear to the door. Is Dad home? Who is he with? I insert my key in the lock and push the door open ever so slightly.

Two people sit close together on the couch, talking and drinking beer.

Theo and Plum.

I stifle a swear. "*What* is going on?"

Theo twists around in his seat and smirks at me. "Yo, Bumblebee. Bet you didn't think you'd see me here, huh?"

Plum glares at me and doesn't say a word.

Cream Puff trots up to me, meowing and purring; I guess she doesn't realize that my world just blew up in my face.

God, I was an idiot to think that my Theo alibi was fool-proof. "Plum. Hey. What are you doing here?" I manage feebly.

Plum crosses her arms over her chest. "Really, Bea? You're asking *me* to explain why *I'm* here, when you're the one who has a mountain of explaining to do?"

"Yes, I know, and I'm really, really—"

"For your information, I came over to give you a bunch of souvenirs I picked up for you in Boston. College catalogs, T-shirts, bumper stickers. Cookies from Aunt Jessika. Plus, I was worried about you because you weren't reading or answering my texts. I thought that maybe you'd lost your phone."

"It died, and I forgot to pack my charger." I don't add that I was too distracted to bother buying a new one.

Plum opens her mouth, then clamps it shut again and shakes her head. I realize then that her eyes are red and that her cheeks are blotchy. Has she been crying? Did *I* do that?

Of course I did that. I am the lamest, most selfish friend in the world.

Theo rises from the couch and stretches. "Your adorable friend here dropped by while I was watching the game. She told me the whole story about how I'm dying and all. She was pretty upset. Good thing I was here to comfort her." He winks at Plum. "You want another beer, gorgeous?"

Plum tilts her head up to him. "Yes, please."

I stare at them in shock. What does he mean, "comfort"? Are they flirting? Is my brother actually hitting on Plum?

"Theo, *stop* it! She's seventeen!" I yell at him.

He ignores me and heads for the kitchen.

Plum tosses her hair over her shoulders and seethes at me.

"Can I talk to you? Alone?" I ask her.

"No!"

"I have something really important to tell you. *Please.*"

"*Fine.* Five minutes. Then I'm leaving."

"Great! Thank you! Come with me!"

I take her hand and lead her up the stairs. Cream Puff follows at our heels. When we get to my room, I close the door and lock it so that Theo can't interrupt us.

Plum perches on the edge of my bed and peers around curiously. It occurs to me that she hasn't been to my house in a really long time.

"Plum, did he . . . did my brother try anything?" I ask cautiously.

"What do you mean?"

"You know he's almost thirty years old, right?"

"And you're in a position to be judgmental about that, why?"

"That's different. Dane's only twenty-seven, and besides, we're . . . I'm . . . "

"You're what?"

The reality of Dane and me hits me with the force of a thousand shooting stars.

"I think I'm falling in love with him," I confess.

"*Excuse* me?"

"We went to New York City together this weekend. That's what I wanted to tell you. We—" I break into a huge smile and lower my voice. *"We had sex."*

"Whaaaat?" Plum gapes at me with a shell-shocked expression. "I thought . . . But I asked you, and you said you had that

moment at the café with him, but that was it, and . . ."

"I know. I'm sorry. But things have been building up between us, and he's completely paranoid about people finding out. He swore me to secrecy." Which is kind of the truth, except that he and I didn't have that conversation until just yesterday. "He wanted to take me to New York City this weekend to play for his teacher at Juilliard. That super-famous concert pianist. It was literally the only free time she had all fall. I played for her, and she wants me to be her student! Isn't that *amazing*?"

"Wait. Hold up. You want to become a professional musician all of a sudden?"

"No, not all of a sudden. It's something I've always dreamed of."

"And you chose not to share this with me?"

"I couldn't. I couldn't even admit it to myself."

"Why not?"

It takes me a long time to tell her the whole story. Everything, even the part about my mom dying right after I was born. I can't seem to utter the exact words "amniotic fluid embolism," but she gets the idea anyway. We both start crying at that part, although she doesn't reach out to bear hug me, like she normally, absolutely would.

"I thought there was no way I could become a pianist," I finish. "But Dane changed all that. He changed my whole life. He encouraged me to pursue music. He said I was good enough, more than good enough. He gave me tons of private lessons to help me prepare for my meeting with Annaliese. And now that I've played for her and seen Juilliard . . . well . . . I definitely want to apply there. I want to go to a conservatory, Plum."

"Oh. My. God." Plum flops back onto the bed. "An hour ago I never wanted to see your face again. And now this."

"I know. I'm so, so sorry."

"Does Kit Harrington know we're having this conversation?"

"*No!* And you have to swear you won't say a word to anyone. *Promise* me."

"I promise. Hey, Bea?"

"What?"

"I'm really glad you told me about your mom."

"Yeah. Me too."

"But that doesn't mean we're okay."

"I know."

"Honestly, I should never speak to you again."

"I know."

We lie there for a long time in silence.

Cream Puff jumps onto the bed and nestles herself between us, purring.

THIRTY-TWO

After Plum leaves, I go downstairs and clean up Theo's many beer bottles. He left at some point while Plum and I were having our heart-to-heart.

Then I return to my room and putter around. When I find my charger and plug in my phone, thirty new voice and text messages pop up—all from Plum, all from over the weekend.

Yikes, I really *was* a bad friend.

I sit down at my desk and turn on my computer. Cream Puff settles down on my lap. So much has happened, and I feel overwhelmed. Good-overwhelmed because of Dane, plus my conversation with Plum. Bad-overwhelmed because I still have to have that same conversation, minus the Dane part, with Dad.

Also, what is Theo up to with Plum? Or does he always act like that around cute girls, women, whatever? In some ways I really don't know him at all. Before he left for college, he was always drunk and getting into trouble and yelling a lot. Dad *tried* to be a parent, I think, sort of, but that obviously didn't work out, and I think he gave up after a while. He and Theo barely speak to each other now.

Theo was twelve when Mom died and Dad abandoned us to have his marathon nervous breakdown. I have a wisp of a memory of me being a toddler and Theo crying on the phone and begging Dad to come back to us.

Obviously, Theo still totally blames me for everything. Maybe he always will.

The front door opens and shuts with a rattling of keys. "Beatrice?"

"I'm up here, Dad!"

Footsteps trudge up the stairs. A minute later Dad knocks, pokes his head into my room, and walks in. He is carrying his briefcase in one hand and a Dunkin' Donuts cup in the other. His clothes are wrinkled, as though he slept in them, and a coffee stain blooms across his polo shirt.

"Hey, honey. When did you get back?" he asks with a weary smile.

"A little while ago."

"So what did you think of Cambridge?"

"Actually . . . " I hesitate. Maybe I should ease into the

subject of New York City and Juilliard gradually, especially since I haven't figured out how to explain Dane to Dad yet. "Cambridge was nice. Really, um, collegiate."

"Did you get to that coffee shop I mentioned? In Kendall Square? It was a big MIT hangout. I used to spend a lot of time there in my undergrad days."

"Nope, we ran out of time. Next trip, though."

Cream Puff leaps off my lap and prances over to Dad. She weaves through his legs, meowing.

He squats down and sets his briefcase aside to pet her. "Yeah, I know. You need to be brushed. Hey, I picked up some cans of that fishy stuff you like," he tells her.

I blink. Dad and Cream Puff are bonding? Did aliens take over his body?

He straightens up and massages his left shoulder. "Say, I've been meaning to ask you: Is there something I can do to help you with your college applications? It's been a while, but I could edit or proofread or whatnot."

First the cat. Now he's showing interest in my life. This is getting more and more surreal.

"Thanks, Dad. I'll let you know."

"Alrighty. I've got a couple calls to make. If you're hungry, there's chili in the fridge. Hannah dropped by yesterday with a big pot."

"That was nice of her."

"Yeah, don't know what we'd do without our Hannah."

He starts to leave. But before he does, he scans my room in a quick, furtive way, as though I might catch him looking. His gaze lands briefly on my blue bookshelf with the sea horses, and he pinches the bridge of his nose. He looks so old suddenly—even older than usual, that is.

And then it occurs to me: The bookshelves must remind him of Mom. Were they hers?

"Hey, Dad?"

"Yeah, honey?"

I'm not sure what I want to say here. *What's up? When did you start liking cats? Are you feeling okay?*

"Do you care where I go to college? I mean, like, do you have an opinion?" I ask him cautiously.

"No. Of course not. You should choose whatever school makes you happy."

"Really?"

"Why? Do you know where you'd like to go?"

"Um, actually, that's something I've been meaning to talk to you about. Maybe we could go out for pizza sometime and discuss a bunch of stuff?"

Dad nods. "Sure! Just let me know when."

"Okay."

"It's a plan, then."

He picks up his briefcase and walks out of my room. Cream Puffs trails after him.

Definitely surreal . . . but in a good way.

Maybe this Juilliard business is going to work out after all.

I stay up late to pore over the Juilliard website. I grab a piece of paper and jot down the important information: application deadline, requirements for the prescreening recording, and the additional requirements for the live audition. *If* I get a live audition. For the recording I will have to play my Beethoven sonata, the Schumann Fantasy, and a Chopin étude. The live audition calls for more pieces; I look over the list and decide that I could play the Bach Partita, the Rachmaninoff "Little Red Riding Hood" étude, and maybe the Prokofiev sonata or Ravel's "Jeux d'eau." Dane told me on the drive home that these auditions last only ten or twenty minutes and that the judges usually ask the candidates to play just a portion of each piece.

I also check out the websites of the other conservatories Dane mentioned: the Curtis Institute of Music in Philadelphia, the New England Conservatory in Boston, the Peabody Conservatory in Baltimore, and the Manhattan School of Music. I grab another piece of paper and jot down more notes.

My hand flies across the page, and my notes are a manic mix of abbreviations, smiley faces, stars, and exclamation points.

It occurs to me that I'm actually excited about college for the first time since . . . ever.

It occurs to me, too, that I'm starting my Golden Notebook for real. Smiling, I find my stapler and staple the pages together. It's not as pretty as Plum's notebook with its sparkly gold cover. But it's a start.

THIRTY-THREE

I don't see Dane again until Tuesday at chamber rehearsal. When he walks into the room, my knees immediately go weak. I always thought that was a made-up thing, knees going weak, but apparently, I was mistaken. I sit down on the piano bench and pretend to busy myself with some sheet music so I don't faint or fall over or whatever.

Is this what love feels like?

He and I glance at each other briefly as he sets his bag down on one of the desks. His lips twitch in a hint of a smile. I smile back, hyper-aware that Braden and Lianna are standing just a few feet away.

It is intoxicating and also impossible, carrying around this secret. I have no idea how we are going to pull off "professional and platonic" until December.

I hope some distance will help. Just this morning I filled

NANCY OHLIN

out a form in the principal's office to drop music history. I explained that I had too many classes, and they said it would be okay to withdraw from the class so late in the semester as long as I promised to make it up with an art elective next semester. And I know Dane plans to tell our group today that he'll be stepping down as coach. Which means that very soon our contact at school will be all but nonexistent.

"Dane! How was your weekend?" Lianna trills.

"It was fine, thank you, Lianna," Dane says briskly. "Listen, I need to speak to you all about something."

Lianna and Braden exchange a glance. I pretend to study my nails.

"From now on, I want you all to rehearse on your own, without me," Dane goes on. "I have other groups that are really struggling and require more of my time. We can do a couple of final run-throughs, perhaps the week of the holiday concert, and I can offer any last-minute comments then."

"But, *Dane*! We *need* you," Lianna complains.

"You guys are so good, you've made me obsolete," Dane banters lightly.

"Mr. R, do you mean starting today or starting next rehearsal?" Braden asks.

"Today. Right now. I have to be . . . I have to go now and

197

check in on another group. Braden, can I count on you to lead the rehearsals?"

"No problem."

"Right, then." Dane gives a little wave, picks up his messenger bag, and heads for the door. I continue studying my nails while watching him leave out of the corner of my eye.

Braden turns to me. "Did *you* know about this?"

I startle. "Me? No. Why would I?"

"Because, um, you two seem kind of tight."

"What's that supposed to mean?"

Lianna arches her eyebrows. "Yes, Braden, what *is* that supposed to mean? If Dane was picking favorites, he would most definitely pick me. He wrote my rec letter for the conservatories, and I happened to see a copy. He *adores* me."

"Yeah, right, Lianna. You happened to see a copy," Braden says skeptically.

"I *did*! 'Lianna Morrissey is one of the best young musicians I have ever had the privilege to work with,' " she recites with air quotes. "Curtis will be all over that. So will Eastman, Jacobs, and Juilliard."

"You're applying to Juilliard? My friend Trai told me there's only going to be two, maybe three violin openings for next fall. Hardly anyone's graduating this year," Braden says.

"Well, my audition is going to blow the judges away. What

about you, Bea? Are you applying to conservatories too?"

My brain is still stuck on *adores* and *Juilliard.* "Um, maybe?"

"Maybe? Sweetie, the deadlines are, like, six weeks away. Most of us have been preparing our auditions for, like, a whole year."

"I'll be fine. Hey, guys, let's get this rehearsal started, or we'll be here all night. Braden, what do you think? From the top?"

"Sounds good."

We run through the Rachmaninoff once, twice, three times. Braden is surprisingly good at keeping us together and also diffusing Lianna's prima donna complaints: too fast, too slow, too much piano and cello, and so forth. As we rehearse, I mentally scroll through the calendar. October, then November, then December . . . in ten weeks the holiday break will begin. Dane won't be my teacher anymore. And I will have turned eighteen.

We just need to stay away from each other for ten weeks.

Ten weeks.

I need to learn patience. I wonder if I can Google how to do that?

When I get home that night, a text pops up on my phone:

It was hard seeing you.

My heart skips a beat. *It was hard seeing you too*, I write back.

I wait for another text, but . . . nothing. Also, he made me promise that I would delete our conversations, just in case.

I'm not sure why he's being so scrupulous. Like anyone is going to see our texts.

Still, I promised. Reluctantly, I hit the Clear All button.

THIRTY-FOUR

November. More than a month has gone by since New York City, and I feel as though I may lose my mind.

Thanksgiving looms on the horizon. The halls are decorated with turkey lino prints from Mr. Nachtman's art class and bright green posters about the holiday concert. As I head over to the performance arts wing for a rehearsal with Braden and Lianna, I instinctively look for Dane's face in the crowd. He's been out sick for a week, and this is his first day back, or that's what he texted me, anyway. Now that I'm not in music history anymore and he no longer coaches our trio, I hardly ever see him. Just a few times passing each other in the hallway . . . and once, I accidentally-on-purpose brushed my arm against his, and he flinched as though I had burned him and hurried away.

He has e-mailed me about my prescreening recording—very official-sounding e-mails, nothing personal. He also arranged for me to record my pieces at a professional studio in Eden Grove this Saturday, although he said he couldn't be there because he has to go out of town.

He still texts me, but those texts have become more and more rare. And once I delete them, it's like they never existed.

Our relationship has become a ghost in my head, gossamer and untouchable. Did New York City really happen?

At least things are better with Dad. He and I finally had that talk—not the whole talk, because I didn't mention Dane or the New York City trip, but the "I think I may want to study music at college" talk. He took it a lot better than I thought he would. We didn't have some cathartic father-daughter moment; he didn't hug me and say, *I'm so proud of you, honey,* which is what normal, not-crazy parents do. But he didn't start sobbing or screaming at me, so I figure that's a minor victory.

Of course, I didn't elaborate that I want to go to a *conservatory* for college. And neither of us uttered the word "Juilliard." One step at a time.

Things are better with Plum, too. She has finally forgiven me for lying to her and for bailing on our Boston weekend. This past Monday she even brought me a pickle and barbecue sauce sandwich at lunch. She also invited me over for *doro wat* for the first time in forever.

I keep telling myself to just be grateful. I have a purpose

and a direction, finally. Dad isn't being insane. Plum and I are getting along again.

Still. What if Dane has changed his mind about us? *Then* what?

After our rehearsal Braden and Lianna take off for other appointments. I start to leave too, then decide to stay and practice the Schumann Fantasy for a bit while I have access to a real piano. I've gotten spoiled with the brand-new Steinway, and now it's hard for me to tolerate my old, out-of-tune upright at home.

I lock the door, even though no one seems to be around at this late hour, and dim the lights. I sit down on the bench and begin.

Only a few measures in, I feel the visceral connection, the familiar joy, kick in. This music and this piano belong together. I never quite realized how much the upright was holding me back. On a good piano, especially this piano, the Fantasy sounds like an entirely different piece, full of nuances and undercurrents and dimensions of color.

I finish the first movement, then the second. As I start the third, I try to remember what Dane taught me. Let go and interpret the music with my heart, not my head. Close my eyes and breathe and *just play.*

He once said that artists aren't like other people, that

they shouldn't abide by rules and preconceived notions.

I imagined that he was talking about *us*.

In the middle of the third movement I hear a key rattling in the lock. My hands fumble and collapse on an A-minor chord as I turn to see who it is.

Oh my God, it's *him*.

Heat rises to my cheeks. "Hey! Hi! I was just thinking about . . . um . . . How are you?" I call out awkwardly.

Dane hovers in the doorway. "I heard you playing. Your Schumann. It sounds incredible."

"Thank you."

We stare at each other. His face is pale, and his olive trench coat hangs loosely on his frame. Has he lost weight?

"Are you . . . okay?" I ask tentatively.

"I'm fine. Just this . . . I had the flu or something."

"I'm glad you're better."

"Yes, me too." He glances around the room. "Stupid of me, I got all the way home before I realized that I'd forgotten my bag. I think I left it in here somewhere."

"Oh!"

He doesn't move from the doorway, though, but instead continues to study me with an expression I can't decipher. Misery. Happiness. Confusion. Maybe he hasn't changed his mind about us after all?

I try to look composed, but it's an effort because my heart is pounding in my chest like an out-of-control metronome. God, he is so beautiful. And sexy. The memory of New York City comes flooding back, and I have to turn away and flip through some random score, Broadway show tunes, so he doesn't see how frazzled I am.

"Well, I'm just going to grab my . . . ," I hear him say.

"Yeah, I should go too."

"I didn't mean to interrupt you. Why don't you finish your practicing?"

"Um, okay."

"Could I . . . maybe I could stay a bit and listen to you? It's been a while. Maybe I could offer you some, you know, advice."

"Really?"

"Really."

He sits down at one of the student desks and adjusts his tall frame to fit the small space. The hem of his trench coat grazes the floor. It's been so long since we've done this—been in the same room, discussed and played music—that I feel positively giddy with pleasure. I also feel guilty because we're breaking the rule we made for ourselves, except that no one knows about that rule except for us, so it's a thrilling sort of guilty.

"Beatrice?"

"Sorry! Just trying to find my beginning."

"Of course. Sorry."

I start the Fantasy from the top. As I play, I can feel Dane watching me intently, which makes me attack the piece with greater fervor. I now understand how Schumann must have felt, weaving a passionate love letter out of music because he couldn't be with the object of his desire.

Complex. Not straightforward. Intense love and longing. Unattainable.

When I reach the final chord of the piece—the final *two* chords, which are identical and marked *pppp*—I caress the keys so lightly and tenderly that they are barely audible. As my hands melt away, a quiet ecstasy ripples through me.

After a long moment I glance up to see Dane's reaction.

I recognize the burning, hungry look.

"Dane," I whisper.

A muscle works in his jaw. "I'd better go. It was foolish of me to stay."

"I'm sorry!"

"I'm sorry too. This is more difficult than I thought it would be."

"I know."

We stand up at the same time. Our eyes meet.

Then something shifts, and we rush toward each other. He wraps me in his arms and crushes me against his body. We kiss.

"Beatrice," he murmurs, his lips moving down my neck. He begins to unbutton my blouse.

"Dane . . . no."

But we can't seem to stop. He touches me; I touch him; we moan and shudder. My blouse flutters to the floor, and his hands are everywhere, making my skin prickle with fire.

At one point he steps away from me just long enough to turn the lights off completely and check to see that the door is locked.

This is a bad, bad idea, I think.

But still, we don't stop.

Thirty-Five

The next day, eighth period, I walk through the performing arts wing on my way to study hall. New motivational posters cover the walls: BELIEVING IN YOURSELF IS THE FIRST STEP TO SUCCESS! . . . DO WHAT YOU'RE AFRAID OF . . . CREATE YOUR FUTURE. But I'm in such a good mood that they don't make me cranky like they normally would.

Actually, I can't seem to stop smiling.

We promised each other it wouldn't happen again. He apologized for getting carried away. I apologized too. He said it was his fault, though, because he was the adult and he should have known better, had more self-control.

I reminded him that I would be an adult, too, next month. Which is both wonderful and surreal. On December fifteenth I will be a child. On December sixteenth I will be an adult. I don't understand how that works, but no matter . . . the important thing is that after the sixteenth I can do whatever I want and be with whomever I want.

Until then, I need to concentrate on my conservatory applications, anyway.

In the meantime, we swore we would stay away from each other at school. Like, *really* stay away.

Still . . . I can't resist stopping in the hall and backing up a few steps to the door of the music history room. I peer through the glass pane, just for a quick glimpse. Or maybe I can even catch his eye. Just looking can't hurt, right?

A gray-haired man is standing at the blackboard.

My smile quickly vanishes. Who is that? He picks up a piece of chalk and writes: *Mr. Pashke.*

He must be a substitute; maybe Dane is sick again. I reach into my pocket and pull out my phone so I can text him.

Someone taps me on the shoulder. "Excuse me."

It's Miss Haskell, one of the school secretaries. "The principal would like to see you," she says primly.

"I'm sorry, what for?"

"He didn't say. Just come with me, please."

Too much is happening at once. Confused, I tuck my phone back into my pocket and follow Miss Haskell down the hall. What is going on? Where is Dane? And why does Principal Oberdorfer want to see me?

His office is on the opposite side of the building. It's actually a network of offices, with secretaries and other adminis-
trative types whose jobs seem to consist of creating paperwork
and being cheerfully unhelpful to people on the phone. Miss
Haskell leads me to a door at the far end. There is a brown-
and-gold plaque next to it: FRANCIS J. OBERDORFER, PRINCIPAL.

Inside, Principal Oberdorfer is talking to a police officer.

What the . . . ?

The two men rise to their feet. "Ah, there you are, Miss
Kim. Come in, come in. This is Detective Torres," Principal
Oberdorfer says, introducing us.

"H-hello."

Detective Torres nods curtly at me. My head spins with
worry. Has Dad been in an accident? Or Theo? Has Theo
been *arrested*? There was that time in ninth grade when he was
picked up for shoplifting.

Miss Haskell leaves, closing the door behind her. Principal
Oberdorfer points to a chair, and I sit down.

"Is my family okay?" I blurt out, unable to contain my anxiety.

"What? Yes, of course, your family is just fine. Candy?"
Principal Oberdorfer pushes a crystal bowl across his desk.

Candy? "No, thank you."

"Detective Torres would like to ask you some questions
about a certain matter."

I swivel in my chair to face the other man. "Yes?"

Detective Torres reaches for a small notebook and flips it open. "So. Miss Kim. Earlier today a student came forward alleging that you and Mr. Rossi engaged in sexual activity last night. Here at school, in one of the classrooms."

He gazes steadily at me and waits for my reaction. Panic freezes my brain. Someone *saw* us?

I swallow and try to recover my equilibrium. *Make something up,* I tell myself, but my thoughts are in complete turmoil.

"Miss Kim?" Detective Torres prompts me.

"I . . . I'm sorry, I'm kind of in shock right now. This is . . . it's insane. Who told you? They're lying."

"So you're saying that this witness's account is untrue?" Detective Torres presses. He clicks on a pen and scribbles something in his notebook.

"It's totally untrue. *Ugh.* Mr. Rossi is my teacher. He helps me with my piano music. That's *all.*" Now the lies are flowing more smoothly.

"Were you in the performing arts wing last night around six, six thirty? In Room 124? I believe people refer to it as the music history room?"

"I'm not sure about the exact time, but yes. Our trio was wrapping up our rehearsal. We're playing Rachmaninoff in the holiday concert."

"Was Mr. Rossi present at this rehearsal?"

"No. It was just me and Lianna and Braden. Lianna Morrissey and Braden Hunt."

"Did you stay on in the music history room after the rehearsal was over? After Lianna and Braden left?"

I manage a casual shrug. "Just for a little while, to practice."

"Did Mr. Rossi happen to stop by while you were practicing?"

"Just for a minute. He forgot his bag. But seriously, nothing happened. That's just gross. Who is this 'witness,' anyway?" I try to sound annoyed, even a little indignant.

"We're not at liberty to say. But we will be investigating this matter further." Detective Torres slaps his notebook shut, tucks it into his back pocket, and stands up. "Thank you for your time, Miss Kim. I'll let you know if I have any other questions."

"Sure, anytime. Nice meeting you."

Detective Torres doesn't budge; he and Principal Oberdorfer must want to talk in private. I force myself to smile as I get up from my chair and leave.

As I head into the deserted hallway, my pulse throbs in my ears. Did they believe my story? Dane won't be arrested, will he?

I find my phone and text Dane with trembling fingers: *Do you know that the police are asking about us?*

A moment later he texts back: *I will ring you later. Please don't try to contact me in any way. Will explain. Delete immediately.*

Oh, God. What is going on?

A sickening feeling fills my chest.

THIRTY-SIX

As soon as the dismissal bell sounds, I grab my stuff from my locker, rush into the parking lot, and call Dane. He doesn't answer. I send him a couple more texts, too, but he doesn't answer those, either. I know he said no contact, but I can't help it—I have to know what's happening.

And then suddenly, I get paranoid that the police seized his phone. I've seen it on TV, and I'm pretty sure they do it in real life, too.

I decide to go to his house. I know that qualifies as "contact," but there's no other way. Besides, his house is set way back from the street, and he has a tall fence around his yard and lots of trees, so no one will see me there.

Determined, I start down School Spirit Boulevard. As I walk, I text Plum to say that I won't be able to come over tonight. I need to talk to her about what happened, but that will have to wait. A moment later she texts back that she has to work on her applications anyway. She adds that her dad is making Swedish food for dinner, off schedule since he usually does that on Tuesdays, and did I want to stop by later for that?

Swedish food is seriously the last thing on my mind.

I hurry my footsteps, ignoring the cars rushing by and the crowds of carefree, chattering students walking as one toward downtown. On the median the maples have lost their leaves and turned into thin brown skeletons.

Gnarled old trees. My first time at Dane's house, when things between us were still unspoken . . . when he was just my teacher. How can a relationship that was so magical and exciting turn into *this*? Into pure awfulness?

My phone buzzes, startling me. I check the screen and the words "Unknown Number" come up.

I answer hastily. "Hello?"

"Beatrice."

"Dane?" His voice is so strained, I barely recognize it.

"Yes, it's me. Are you alone?"

"Yes! Oh my God, are you all right? I'm on my way to your house."

"*No!* Beatrice, listen to me. You absolutely *cannot* come over. I'm not at home anyway."

"Where are you calling from?"

"I borrowed a friend's mobile. Have the police talked to you?"

"Yes. Miss Haskell pulled me out of eighth period. Dane, what's going on?"

"Tell me everything you told the police. Please. From the beginning."

"O-okay."

I spot an empty bench, brush off some dead leaves, and sit down. It's cold out, a damp November cold, but I hardly notice. I take a deep breath, then recount my conversation with Detective Torres to Dane, word for word.

"Is that all? Nothing else?" he says when I finish.

"Nothing else. Dane, who *saw* us?"

"I don't know. But I need you to listen to me carefully."

"You're scaring me."

"Don't be scared. Just listen."

"Yes, okay."

"This morning Principal Oberdorfer summoned me into his office. He told me about what this witness said. I denied it, of course; I said it was preposterous. He said he was obligated to report it to the police anyway. I'm on my way to the station now; they want to interview me there."

"They're not going to arrest you, are they?" I cry out.

"I don't know. I hope not. But for now, though, we need to get our stories straight."

"What do you want me to say?"

For the next half hour we comb over every last detail of our time together: Music history classes. Chamber rehearsals. Café Tintoretto. Our private lessons. Even New York City. By the time we are through, we have a coherent narrative in place as well as a plan of action, sort of.

"One more thing," Dane adds. "My solicitor has advised me that you and I should stay away from each other for a while. So from now on, no calls, no e-mails, no texts. And definitely no visits."

"Your solicitor?"

"My lawyer."

I feel myself start to shake. "Oh my God, Dane. So this is really serious."

"Yes, it's very serious. Last night . . . it was very stupid of me to . . . I don't know what I was . . . "

He doesn't say anything else.

I can barely hold on to my phone, my hands are shaking so badly. How could this have happened? Dane has been nothing but wonderful to me. Also, we care about each other. We may even be in love. . . .

"Beatrice, I need to go. Just so you know, I won't back

to school for a while. Principal Oberdorfer wants this issue resolved first."

"O-okay."

"I'll ring you again when I can. Find Braden and talk to him, like we discussed. Your friend Plum, too. We'll get through this."

The line goes dead.

Now my whole body is shaking.

Get through this . . . *how?*

I call Plum immediately.

"What do you think are my strengths and my weaknesses?" she asks when she picks up.

In response, I burst into tears.

"Bea! Oh my gosh, what's wrong?"

"Everything! My life is falling apart."

"What do you mean?"

I tell her the whole story.

"You had *sex* in his *classroom?*"

"It was crazy, I know. We just . . . we got carried away. But apparently, someone saw us. And now the police are investigating."

"Oh my gosh, what can I do?"

"If the police ask you, can you tell them that you were with me the few times I went over to Dane's house for piano lessons?"

"Got it. You'll have to tell me dates and stuff, though. And what his house looks like. And if he has pets. He seems like a cat person. And—"

"I'll call you again later tonight. Or I'll stop by, if I can. Right now I have to find Braden."

"The violin guy?"

I am too upset to bother correcting her. "Yeah, the violin guy. Dane wants me to ask him to cover for us too."

THIRTY-SEVEN

It's strange, going to Café Tintoretto without Dane. But it was the first place I thought of when I told Braden that I needed to see him ASAP.

When I walk into the café, Signor Vitale waves to me from behind the counter. The silver urn is hissing steam, and the air smells like coffee beans. "*Ciao, signorina.* You have returned! Where is the *professore*?"

"I'm meeting a friend. May I have a cappuccino?" I ask with a tight smile.

"*Si, arrive subito.* Coming right up."

When I turn around to find an empty table, I see that Braden is already here, sipping at an iced something and scrolling through his phone. His cello case, covered with stickers, is propped up against the wall. Did he overhear the *professore* comment? I smooth my hair and try not to look nervous as I hurry over to join him.

He glances up from his phone and beams at me. "Hey, Bea!"

"Hey, Braden. Thanks for coming on such short notice."

"Well, you did say that we should go out for coffee sometime."

"I did? Oh, yeah, I did. Listen, Braden. I have a favor to ask you."

Disappointment flickers in his eyes. "Ah! The favor. And here I was, thinking we were on a date."

"Well, ironically, we kind of are."

"I don't follow."

We fall silent as Signor Vitale delivers my cappuccino along with a plate of biscotti. *"Buon appetito!"*

"Grazie."

"You speak Italian?" Braden asks when we are alone again.

"Yeah, like two words. Um, about that favor. I need you to . . . this is really awkward . . . I need you to pretend to be my boyfriend for a while."

I wait for a knee-jerk barrage of questions: *Why? What for? Is this some kind of joke?* But instead, Braden gives me an odd look. "Yeah, I know what this is about."

"You do?"

"Last night. You and Mr. R's X-rated duet in the music history room."

I gape at him.

"Some people were talking about it today," Braden explains.

"They *were?*"

"Yeah. I wonder if Lianna's the one who saw you guys?"

"Lianna?"

I sag back in my chair and stare blankly at the stained-glass window. Ruby, emerald, sapphire. How could Lianna have seen anything? How could *anyone* have seen anything? The room was pitch-black. The door was locked.

"Look," I say, turning back to Braden, "nothing happened between Mr. Rossi and me."

"Nothing, really?"

"No, of *course* not! How can you even ask me that? And why do you think it was Lianna who went to Principal Oberdorfer?"

Braden shrugs. "You know she doesn't like you, right? You're a way better musician than she is. And/or she was angling for the job of teacher's pet, and then you came along."

"I am not Mr. Rossi's—"

"Don't worry. I get that you and Mr. R have a very Shostakovich-Nikolayeva relationship. Actually, maybe more like Pogorelich-Kezeradze."

"What does that even mean?"

"Doesn't matter. I'll help you."

"You will?"

"Yeah, why not? I'm a nice guy."

He smiles at me in this rueful way, and for a brief moment I flash back to summer: the two of us making out in the backseat of his car, wasted from the bottle of red wine that I swiped from Dad's liquor cabinet. I remember the sweat pouring off our bodies—we were in the middle of a heat wave—and the bright, tiny fireflies that punctuated the darkness outside. The air was thick with heat and honeysuckle. Most of our clothes were off, and we came *this close* to going all the way.

But at the last minute, just as he was reaching for the condoms, I had a panicky change of heart. I have no idea why; it just felt *wrong*. He was really understanding about it, even the next day, when I told him that I wanted to go back to being just friends.

My life would be so much easier if I dated guys like Braden . . . guys my own age.

"So what's the plan?" Braden prompts me.

"Um, so . . . if anyone asks, like the police or Principal Oberdorfer or whoever, can you tell him that we're together? That we've been in a relationship since, like, the beginning of summer?"

"Is this to make them believe you're hooking up with me and not Mr. R?"

I blush. "Yeah, that's the idea."

"Have we said 'I love you' to each other, or have we not gotten there yet?"

"Um, sure."

"I'll need some more details about us. I'll start a notebook so I can keep track. Oh, and we should definitely go to the homecoming dance together."

"Um, I guess?"

"Roses or orchids?"

"Excuse me?"

"Your corsage. Would you prefer roses or orchids?"

I wish he didn't sound so enthusiastic about all this.

THIRTY-EIGHT

When I get home, I find Dad sitting on the couch, nursing a scotch in the dark.

I flick on the overhead light. "Dad?"

As soon as he turns to look at me, I know that he knows.

Oh my God, I am in So. Much. Trouble.

"I've been trying to get hold of you, Bea. Your principal called me," he says in a steely voice.

"Oh."

I take off my jacket and hang it up in the closet, biding my time. I can hear Cream Puff in the kitchen, meowing and batting her bowl around.

"I think Cream Puff needs her dinner—," I begin.

"Later. Sit down, please."

"Okay." I perch on the far end of the couch and don't meet his eyes. A long, terrible silence hangs between us. I stare at the wood floor and notice a big, jagged scratch. How long has it been there?

Dad finally speaks. "Beatrice, I need you to tell me about this Mr. Rossi." He calls me by my full name only when he's angry.

"W-what about him?"

"Did he . . ." He falters. "Did this man *molest* you?"

The word "molest" cuts like a knife. "God, *no!*"

"Then *what*?"

"Really, this is all just a big misunderstanding."

"Explain it to me, then."

"Yes, okay."

I decide to recycle the story I told Braden earlier and add in the detail about Lianna, even though it's probably false. "This girl at school . . . I think she may have lied and said some stuff about me and Mr. Rossi. None of it's true. I told Principal Oberdorfer that, and the policeman, too."

"You mean Detective Torres?"

"Wait, how do you know his name?"

"I called up a buddy of mine at the DA's office, and he filled me in."

I twist my hands in my lap. This whole situation is swirling out of control. "The police will drop this, right? They'll realize it's a mistake?" I say hopefully.

"I'm not sure. They'll be wanting to conduct an investigation first, to determine if this is a case of statutory rape."

"*What?* But D—Mr. Rossi didn't rape me. He didn't do *anything* to me."

"But if he did . . . if the two of you had sex, which is what this witness said she saw . . ." Dad hesitates. "The age of consent in this state is eighteen. Which means that you, Bea, aren't able to consent to sex because you're only seventeen. Even if you *think* you consented, even if you said 'yes' a dozen times, even if you're the one who initiated . . . you didn't consent. You *can't.* Therefore, if someone eighteen or over has sex with you, they are guilty of statutory rape and could go to jail for up to ten years."

"*Ten years?* You have *got* to be joking."

"I'm afraid not. In addition, because we don't have what's commonly called a 'Romeo and Juliet provision' in this state, basically no one under eighteen can consent to sex with anyone, regardless of age. The DA could, for example, prosecute two sixteen-year-olds for having sex with each other."

"Are you *serious?* Dad, tons of people in my school are having sex. Everyone *everywhere* is having sex. Are you saying they're all breaking the law?"

"If they're under the age of consent, then, yes."

"God, you sound like a lawyer!"

"I *am* a lawyer. And right now you need to listen to me. Very carefully. This is an extremely serious matter."

I cross my arms over my chest. How can this be happening? I knew Dane and I weren't *technically* allowed to have sex until I was eighteen and he was no longer a teacher at my school. That's why we'd planned to wait until December.

Still, I didn't think he could go to jail. And for *ten years*?

"Bea?"

"What?"

"I need to know. Did you have sex with this man?"

"No!"

"Did he come on to you in any way? Say anything? Touch you?"

"No!"

"Then what is this about?"

"*God!*"

I bend down and put my head in my hands. It's an effort not to start crying or throwing things or whatever. Last night in the music history room was a huge mistake, but it's not like Dane and I did anything immoral. I wanted him, and he wanted me. He's not some sleazy child molester.

"Honey?" Dad says.

"What?"

"Talk to me. *Please.*"

I sniffle and flop back against the couch, wondering what equation of truth and lies I should tell him. Obviously, I can't say as much as I said to Plum. Dad needs to know some of it, though—about the private lessons and maybe the trip to New York City, too.

I brace myself. "Dad."

"Yes, honey?"

"Mr. Rossi . . . he's more than just a teacher to me. He heard me play the piano and said I was a prodigy. He arranged for me to meet with his former teacher at Juilliard, who's a famous concert pianist. He drove me to New York City on Columbus Day weekend, and—"

"Excuse me, he did *what*?" Dad erupts.

I hold up my hands. "I'm sorry. I lied about being in Boston with Plum. But I was worried that if I told you where I was really going, you would say no."

He stares at me in astonishment.

"When you and I went out for pizza a few weeks ago, I told you I wanted to study music at college, right? The thing is, I don't want to go to a regular old college. I want to go to a conservatory. And my first choice is . . . it's Juilliard," I continue.

His face blanches.

"I really want to become a professional musician, like Mom," I rush on. "But I couldn't tell you before because, well . . . it made you so miserable every time I even *touched* the piano. And Mr. Rossi . . . he changed all that, encouraged me to pursue my dreams. He spent hours and hours of his own time teaching me and coaching me and preparing me for my appointment at Juilliard. He believes in me. Why is that so wrong?"

Dad picks up his scotch, twirls the glass in his hand, and sets it down again. A million emotions cross his face, and I don't understand any of them.

"I am so sorry, honey," Dad says finally.

"*You're* sorry? What for?"

"I thought I was doing the right thing by keeping your mom out of your life. I see now that I made a terrible mistake."

"It's okay, Dad."

"No, it's not okay. I'm a rotten father. I knew I couldn't do this without your mom. I've already ruined your brother's life, and—" Tears stream down his cheeks as he turns away from me.

I scoot over and hug him. "It's okay. We'll fix this. We'll fix Theo, too, somehow. Just be our dad, okay?"

He bends his head to my shoulder, crying, and I start crying too.

The grief, the years, have finally caught up to us.

THIRTY-NINE

I can't sleep.

It's the middle of the night, and I'm lying in bed, my mind churning restlessly. Cream Puff is a warm, snoring puddle at my feet. Moonlight slants through the window and illuminates the spines of the books on my blue sea horse shelves. I wish I could call Dane, but I can't because of what the solicitor guy said. I can't call Plum, either, because it's the middle of the night.

Finally, at around three a.m., I get out of bed, walk over to my desk, and boot up my computer. When the screen flickers to life, I type—what was the phrase Dad used?—*age of consent.*

Dozens of links pop up. I open each one and read about the different ages of consent in different places. In Georgia it's sixteen. In Texas it's seventeen. In some states it is as low as thirteen under certain circumstances.

Great. So if I lived in one of these other states, I could legally consent to sex. But because I happen to live here, I can't. That makes zero sense.

I then Google "student" and "teacher" and "affair." My eyes widen when I see the number of news headlines from just the past few months alone. The ages of the students and teachers are all over the place. Fourteen and thirty-three—that's too big of an age difference; plus, fourteen is so young. Fifteen and forty—*definitely* too big. Sixteen and twenty-seven—a little better. Seventeen and twenty-two—much better. Both male and female teachers are represented, as are male and female students. Some of the teachers were arrested and sent to jail; some were simply fired from their jobs.

I click on the stories so I can read them more carefully. That's when I start to feel a bit queasy. A high school fresh-man commits suicide over her broken relationship with her soccer coach. A thirty-five-year-old teacher becomes pregnant by her seventh-grade student. Another thirty-five-year-old teacher makes sex tapes of threesomes with her pupils and shares them with her friends. A tenth grader tries to kill her best friend in a rivalry over their mutual "boyfriend," who is also their history teacher. A twelve-year old-girl tells her parents that her teacher has been "touching" her for months and that they're going to get married someday.

Lives ruined by . . .

Depression and drug abuse . . .

Molestation . . .

Sex offenders . . .

Preying on the innocent and vulnerable . . .

I shut down my computer. None of this applies to Dane and me. I'm not a child. He's not a predator. We *want* to be together.

Still, I do have to admit that these other situations seem creepy and very, very wrong.

I wonder if the kids at A-Jax are even aware of these consent laws. I wasn't joking with Dad when I said that everyone is having sex. Which means that in theory, 90 percent of our student population could be arrested. Including Braden and me, if we had gone through with it last summer. It's ludicrous.

Ten years in jail. No wonder Dane was so freaked out when we spoke on the phone.

I have to protect him, no matter what it takes.

FORTY

Thanksgiving. Theo doesn't come home, which he sometimes does, but instead texts Dad last minute and tells him he's going snowboarding in Vermont with some friends.

So it's just Dad and me and Cream Puff. Dad actually made a turkey, which he's never done before; usually, we just go to a restaurant. My contributions are cranberry sauce, mashed potatoes, and gravy from some recipes I found online.

As we eat, Dad asks me about my Juilliard application. He can finally say the word "Juilliard" without tearing up. "When is it due?"

"In a few days. I have to finish my essay and also upload my recordings."

"What about your other applications?"

"Peabody and the Manhattan School of Music and NEC are the same as Juilliard. Curtis is the middle of December."

"Neck?"

"New England Conservatory of Music."

"Yeah, that's right. Your mom—" He pauses and pinches the bridge of his nose.

"What about Mom?"

"She thought about going there for a graduate degree. But then she got pregnant with Theo."

"Oh. Wow."

We eat our turkey in silence. A football game is on the TV on mute, but neither of us is paying attention. I keep thinking that Dane might call or text me, since it's a holiday, but I realize how absurd that is. I actually haven't heard from him since our strategy session that day when all hell broke loose.

I miss Dane so much, and I am so worried, that I have begun to feel numb. The police have called me in for multiple interviews, but I can't tell if they went well or not. A few times I was tempted to go over to Dane's house and peek in a window, just to make sure he was still there and not in jail. But, lawyer's orders. Besides, I'm supposed to be Braden's girlfriend these days, so I've been hanging out with him a lot after school and pretending to like him *that way*.

I think Braden is starting to take this whole thing way too seriously, though. Yesterday he left a bouquet of flowers on my porch with a note: *Happy Five-Month Anniversary! Love forever, Braden.*

Love forever? Five-month anniversary? Boy, he's really committing to our cover story.

He and Lianna and I have dissolved our trio—or put it on hold, anyway. It just doesn't feel right, under the circumstances. Lianna continues to insist that she didn't turn Dane and me in, contrary to Braden's theory. I'm actually beginning to believe her; she seems sincere for once in her life. But if it wasn't her, who was it?

Dad's phone buzzes with a call. He swipes at his mouth with a paper napkin, glances at the screen, and hits Talk. "Hello?"

He listens intently to someone on the other end. After a few minutes he thanks the person and hangs up.

"Who was that?" I ask curiously.

"Antonio, my friend at the DA's office. He's been keeping me posted on the police investigation, on his own time."

I put my fork down. "And? Dad, *tell* me."

"They've apparently interviewed a lot of people—people at your school, people at a private school where your . . . where Mr. Rossi used to teach," Dad explains. "They can't find anything on him. And without witnesses or evidence, they can't charge him with a crime."

Relief courses through me. "That's good, right? That's *really* good! So he won't be arrested?"

"Not so fast. Antonio said that as of Monday or so, the police were still waiting to hear back from some of the New York City folks. That woman—you know, Mr. Rossi's Juilliard teacher. Also a few others. It's possible the police have wrapped up these interviews already, but Antonio wasn't a hundred percent."

New York City. My mind races through the possibilities: random Juilliard students, the waiter at that French restaurant, the clerk at the motel on Whiterock Beach. The Eden Grove police wouldn't know to track them down. Would they?

And what about Dane's and my alibis? I told Detective Torres that I'd stayed in a youth hostel. Dane told them he'd stayed with friends. Did Dane speak to these "friends" and ask them to cover for him? Did the police contact all the hostels in New York City and inquire about me?

I push away my plate; I've totally lost my appetite.

What if the police manage—managed?—to locate a witness who contradicts my testimony and Dane's?

Early that evening I go over to Plum's house for pumpkin pie. This is another tradition—dessert after our respective Thanksgiving dinners at home, followed by a binge session of old Christmas movies, to transition—but somehow, this year, today, it doesn't feel very festive.

If only the Eden Grove police would fall off the face of the earth.

When I get to the Sorensons', Plum is waiting for me on the front porch. She is bundled up in a ski parka that is several sizes too big for her and thick white Swedish mittens. Next to her is a huge clay pot of orange chrysanthemums and a couple of doggy chew toys.

She smiles and jumps to her feet when she sees me. Then she studies my face, and her smile disappears. "Bea! What's wrong?"

"Nothing. Everything. I don't know," I reply with a shrug.

"Tell me!"

We sit down on the porch together. I recount what Dad's friend at the DA's office told him.

"What if the police found out the truth about New York City and . . ." I shake my head. "They'll arrest him. Dad says he could go to jail for ten years!"

"That's not going to happen," Plum reassures me. "But . . . Bea? There's something else."

"What?"

"I'm sure it's not true, but . . ."

"*What's* not true?"

Plum pulls her knees into her chest swipes at her nose with

the back of her mitten. "Do you remember when I told you about Lakshmi? My neighbor?"

"Who?"

"The one who goes to the Greenley Academy?"

That prep school where Dane used to teach. "Oh, right. What about her?"

"So she's home for Thanksgiving, right? I ran into her this morning, and we got to talking, and I asked her if she knew Kit Harrington—I mean, Mr. Rossi."

"And?"

She drops her gaze to the ground. A cold, sick feeling washes over me.

"Plum? What did Lakshmi say?" I demand.

"She said . . . that her friend at school told her that she and Mr. Rossi had an affair," Plum blurts out.

I flinch as though someone slapped me. I open my mouth to speak, but nothing comes out.

"It's probably made up," Plum rushes on. "Lakshmi said her friend was drunk when she told her, and when Lakshmi asked her about it later, she denied it."

"Yeah, it sounds made up," I manage at last, although my voice sounds far away and hollow.

"The girl's name was Porter something. Porter Caulden. No, Caldwell."

Porter Caldwell.

I gaze up at the sky. The moon looks almost exactly like the one Dane and I saw at Whiterock Beach, a shimmering white wedge. Was that only last month? We made love, we discussed the future.

It can't all have been a lie.

"There's no way Dane did that," I finally say.

"Of course not," Plum agrees, but she won't look at me.

FORTY-ONE

On Friday, I decide to put in a marathon practice session. Plum is finishing up the last of her applications. We're having a sleepover at her house later. In the meantime, I have nothing else to do, and I can't just sit around waiting for Dane to call. Besides, I've been too distracted to practice much lately, and I really need to catch up.

I keep thinking about this Porter Caldwell girl. I actually looked her up on Facebook and Twitter and Instagram, but her accounts were set to private.

I desperately need to talk to Dane, but I can't.

When we do, I'm sure we'll have a big laugh about it. In any case, it's a slippery slope from casual online "research" to jealous freakdom, so I should cut this out already.

Besides, we have *real* problems to worry about, like the police investigation. Dad's DA friend said that Detective

Torres was waiting to hear back from the New York City people. . . .

I sit down at the piano and run through scales. Dad finally had it tuned, for the first time in the fifteen years we've lived here, and it's definitely an improvement. He also told me that Mom's piano still exists and that he would try to get it back for me. Apparently, he loaned it to his alma mater, Columbia University, after she passed away, and it's sitting in one of their parlors.

I click on the gooseneck lamp as I dig through my backpack to find the pieces I need to practice. I decide to begin with the Winter Wind Etude, which I plan to play for my live auditions and which is a study of manual dexterity and flexibility. It's a wild roller-coaster ride of notes up and down the piano that seem to follow no pattern, and it requires balancing the right hand with the left hand in an intricate polyphonic duet.

Closing my eyes, I ease into the first four measures, which are *lento* and melodic and deceptively simple. A beat, a breath . . . then my right hand tears down the keyboard in a rushing cascade of notes, *allegro con brio,* while my left hand maintains the original melody with deep, heavy chords.

When my phone buzzes, I almost don't hear it because I am so wrapped up in the étude.

Dane's number flashes on the screen.

I grab for the phone, fumble it, and pick it up again. "Dane, how are you?" I shout, and I'm out of breath as though I have been running.

He laughs. How can he be laughing?

"I'm fine, love. More importantly, how are you?"

"I'm fine! Well, not fine, exactly, but . . . Where are you? How are you? What's going on? Oh my God, I can't believe it's you!"

"I got a call from Edwin, my solicitor."

I gasp. "Oh no! Is this going to be bad?"

"No, no, it's good. Great, in fact. He just spoke to the police. They're closing the investigation, and they won't be pressing charges."

"What? Really?"

"Really. They can't find anyone or anything to corroborate Braden's story. And without that, they can't prosecute."

"But my dad said they were talking to a bunch of people in New York City. Annaliese and so forth."

"Well, apparently, it was a dead end."

"Oh my God!" And then I do a mental double take. "Wait, did you say . . . *Braden?*"

"Yes. One of the detectives told Edwin that it was Braden who went to Principal Oberdorfer."

"*Braden?* But . . . but . . ."

I squeeze my eyes shut and try to re-create that night. Braden and Lianna left right after our rehearsal. Braden must have come back for some reason and seen Dane and me. But why would he turn us in . . . and then blame it on Lianna?

"I am *so* going to kill him!" I yell.

"Don't. I'm not pleased about it either. But I'm guessing that he thought he was protecting you. Also . . ." Dane hesitates. "I think the bloke might have feelings for you. I've seen the way he looks at you."

"*Feelings?* I don't care, I'm still going to kill him!"

"You should cut him some slack. What's important is that this is over."

"But Braden *started* it."

"No, he didn't. He just complicated things. And in the long run, it all worked out."

"Whatever."

"Beatrice." Dane laughs softly. "Enough about Braden. Please. It's so fantastic to hear your voice. How have you been?"

"It's been . . . I've been—" I stop, not knowing how to explain what I've been going through since the police investigation started. Depressed, miserable, terrified. "I'm fine now. I'm just so relieved that this is over."

"I know. Me too."

"Can I see you?"

"Not right now. But soon, I promise."

"How soon?"

"As soon as Edwin tells me it's all right. For your sake as much as mine."

"Okay, then." It's hard to keep the hurt out of my voice.

"I'm sorry."

"I know. I'm sorry too."

We say good-bye and hang up. This is *good* news, I remind myself. Dane has been cleared. I can stop worrying and lying to everyone and just get on with my life.

So why do I still feel uneasy?

FORTY-TWO

Plum parks her car on Carriage House Lane and turns off the radio—it's '90s night. Somewhere in the distance a dog begins to bark. Across the street a neighbor's curtain flutters in the window.

Plum flips her hair over her shoulder and turns to me. Even in the darkness, I can see the anxious look in her eyes.

"I know, I know," I say before she can lecture me again. "I just need to see him. It won't take long."

"But his lawyer—"

"I know what his lawyer said. But it'll only be for a minute. Five minutes, tops. Then we can go back to your house or go to the movies or whatever you want. Okay? *Please?*"

Plum draws her lips into a thin line.

"I'd do the same thing for you," I say sweetly.

"No, because I would never be in this position, because I would never date a teacher!"

"Liar! What about Mr. Anderson and Mr. Thackeray?"

"They're *fictional*. Fine, go! I'll circle around the block a few times while I'm waiting for you to have your dumb rendezvous."

"Great! Thank you!"

I slide out of the car and watch as she drives off. Tonight was supposed to be a big, fun Friday-night sleepover. But when she picked me up, I asked her to make the detour. I convinced her that it would be safer to have her drive me than for me to take our Subaru, which could be recognized.

The door opens before I even have a chance to knock. Dane stands there, looking absurdly sexy in a blue velvet robe and plaid pajama bottoms.

"Beatrice! I heard someone pull up. What are you doing here?" he asks with a huge smile.

"I wanted to see you."

He takes my hand and pulls me inside. "You're not very good at obeying instructions, are you? On the other hand, I can't tell you how happy I am right this second."

"Really?"

"Really."

Closing the door, he draws me to him and kisses me slowly

and deeply. Relief mingles with desire as I melt into the kiss. He still wants me. Only me. How could I ever have doubted him?

When his lips move down to my neck and then below my neck, I pull back slightly. "Dane!"

"Sorry! It's just that I've missed you."

"I've missed you too. But I can't stay. Plum's driving around the block. I just wanted to . . . I wanted to see you and . . ."

He strokes my hair and kisses me chastely on the cheek. "I know. I promise that soon we can see each other without having to worry about the police, the school, everything."

"Okay."

I turn to go. The space between us feels suddenly cold.

"Dane?"

"What, love?"

"Who's Porter?"

Silence.

I make myself look at him. The color has drained from his face.

Oh, God.

"Dane, who is she? Who's Porter Caldwell?"

"W-where did you hear that name?" he finally manages.

"Plum's neighbor. She goes to Greenley. She told Plum

about the . . . she said that you and this Porter girl may have had an affair."

Dane exhales sharply. "It wasn't an affair."

It wasn't an affair—this was not the answer I wanted to hear.

"It happened once," he goes on. "*Once.* And I didn't know she was a student."

I squeeze my fists and will myself not to cry or scream or slap him. "So I'm not your first one."

"My first . . . ? God, *no,* it wasn't like that! I told you, I didn't know she was a student. Greenley is a very big school. Besides, I didn't meet her there; I met her in New York. I thought she was twenty-one, twenty-two. The way she looked, the way she was tossing back those martinis. I had no idea she was fifteen or that she went to Greenley."

"She was *fifteen*?"

"Yes, and it's not something I'm proud of."

"You had sex with a drunk fifteen-year-old girl," I say incredulously.

"I didn't *know.* I admit, it was colossally stupid of me. I was going through a bad phase in my life. But it's in the past, and it has nothing to do with us."

Nothing to do with us.

I start for the front door again. Dane grabs my arm, and I shake it away roughly.

"Beatrice!"

"I thought you and I . . . but obviously, you have a thing for young girls."

"I do *not* have a 'thing' for young girls. Beatrice, *please*! I was an idiot, and I made a terrible mistake. But my feelings for you aren't based on how old you are. I'd want to be with you whether you were seventeen or twenty-seven or thirty-seven."

"I wish I could believe you."

"Please, love. Can't we talk about this?"

"Not now."

"I'll ring you in the morning, then?"

"I think I just need to be alone for a while."

I hurry outside and close the door behind me. Leaves crunch under my feet, and a gray cloud has settled in front of the moon.

Dane's eucalyptus scent lingers on my skin, and I fight back tears. How could this be happening?

As soon as I get into Plum's car, she knows.

"Ice-cream sundaes or hugs or home?" she asks me immediately.

"All of the above."

"You got it."

As we drive away, I glance over my shoulder at Dane's

house. I can just make out the shadowy outline of his face in the window. Regret and longing pulse through me.

Is this the end? Or just a different beginning?

I wish my love for him had died the exact second he broke my heart.

FORTY-THREE

On the night of my eighteenth birthday, Dad takes Plum and me out to the Crown Club, which is the fanciest restaurant in Eden Grove. We sit in red leather booths, eat shrimp cocktail and massive steaks, and listen to 1950s jazz.

"Wish Theo could have been here," Dad says as he sips at a glass of wine. "I left him a couple messages. I'm surprised he'd turn down a free meal."

"Maybe he's out with his girlfriend?" I suggest.

"Girlfriend, what girlfriend?" Dad asks.

"Valerie something," I say with a shrug. "They seem pretty serious." Which is actually a lie, and I've been trying to turn over a new leaf in the not-lying department. But I need to distract Dad from the fact that Theo has never celebrated my birthday and probably never will. For him, this day is not my birthday, but the anniversary of our mother's death.

Actually, it's kind of a miracle that Dad and I are here. In the past he has barely acknowledged this day; usually it's pizza, store-bought cupcakes, and a Peanuts card with a fifty-dollar bill tucked inside. So . . . progress.

After dinner three tuxedoed waiters bring a massive chocolate cake to our table with an "18" candle in it. Plum sings "Happy Birthday" in an exuberant off-key voice while Dad takes a video with his phone.

"Make a wish!" Plum orders me.

"Okay!"

I scrunch my eyes closed. What should I wish for? What do I want more than anything? *Getting into Juilliard* occurs to me, but for some reason, I can't seem to go there tonight.

I open my eyes and blow out the candle.

"What did you wish for?" Plum asks.

I smile and shrug. "If I tell you, it won't come true."

As we eat cake, I open my presents from Plum: a book called *How to Survive College* and a silver charm bracelet with a piano on it.

"So perfect," I say, hugging her.

"I left my present at home, honey. I'm sorry," Dad apologizes.

The Peanuts card. "No worries, Dad. I'll have something to look forward to," I tell him.

He and Plum check out the college survival book and discuss Cambridge. While they're occupied, I slip my phone out of my purse to see if Dane remembered my birthday.

I haven't seen him since that night. We texted, and I told him that I needed to take a long break from us. I told him that I wasn't sure we could ever be together again.

Still, my heart skips a beat when I see a new message:

Happy birthday.
With all my love,
Dane

I don't delete it.

Dad and I get home around nine, after dropping Plum off at her house. It's a school night, which means that I still have about an hour's worth of homework to do before I can go to bed.

As we walk through the front door, Dad flicks on the living room light and sweeps his arms in a dramatic way. "Ta-da!" he announces.

There is a mahogany Steinway grand where the old upright used to be.

"Oh. My. God." I fling my coat to the floor and rush over

to the piano. I sit down on the padded bench and touch the keys reverently.

"Happy birthday, honey," Dad says with a smile.

"Is this—"

"Yup. Steinway Model L. Built in 1927 in Astoria, Queens, about a mile from where your mom grew up."

"Oh my God."

I take a deep breath and run through some arpeggios. The sound is gorgeous, unlike anything I've ever heard.

Dad brings over a cardboard box and sets it down with a thud. "Found this in the attic. I thought you might like to go through this stuff. There are some other boxes, too."

Curious, I lean over and open the flaps. There is a mountain of sheet music inside: Schumann, Schubert, Liszt, Brahms, and other composers, too. *Natalia Kim* is written on most of the covers, although some of them say *Natalia Levin*. Her handwriting is less curly than it was when she was younger, and she stopped dotting her *i*'s with hearts.

"Dad! This is *amazing*!" I exclaim.

"Yeah, I figured. I've got to . . . I'm going to feed Cream Puff now. You take your time, honey."

He swipes at his eyes and wanders toward the kitchen, the cat at his heels.

I pick up a volume of Chopin nocturnes and leaf through

it. Mom's fingerings and other notations are all over the pages in light pencil.

I continue digging through the box and spot an old book—not a score, but a regular book. Curious, I pull it out. The title is *Testimony: The Memoirs of Dmitri Shostakovich.*

A dried flower falls out of the pages. It is a pink rose, its petals flat and papery and browned with age. I wonder if Dad gave that to Mom?

I open it to a random page and carefully replace the flower. A line in the text catches my eye: *One must speak the truth about the past or not at all.*

I guess Shostakovich knew what he was talking about.

FORTY-FOUR

On the morning of Christmas Eve, I am downtown doing some last-minute shopping when I catch sight of Dane strolling into Café Tintoretto.

I stop in my tracks and stare. Small snowflakes flutter onto my parka and melt into invisible puddles. Nearby, a fake Santa Claus rings his bell to collect money for the Salvation Army.

I haven't seen Dane since the night he told me about Porter Caldwell. His hair is shorter, and I don't recognize his coat, which is dark gray with wide lapels. A blue scarf, also unfamiliar, is wound around his neck. He is carrying the same old messenger bag, though.

I thought I would feel no emotion, but I guess I was wrong. Obviously, it hasn't been long enough. Will it ever be long enough?

On an impulse, I walk up to the café window, which is

adorned with sparkly Christmas lights. Peering inside, I spot Dane at the marble counter talking to Signor Vitale. A moment later he sits down at a table with a cappuccino and reaches into his bag. He pulls out a score and checks his watch.

Is he meeting someone?

I wait for a minute, then two minutes, then three. I'm not sure what I'm doing, watching him through this window—spying, really—but I can't seem to make myself move. I wonder how he is and what he has been up to lately? He never came back to A-Jax, and I didn't return any of his calls or e-mails or texts, even the birthday message, so I have no idea about his life these days.

My breath has formed a faint, foggy circle on the cold glass pane. I wipe it away with my sleeve. Dane is flipping through his score with an expression of great concentration. A lock of hair falls across his forehead, and he pushes it back.

Just then he looks up and sees me.

I jerk back from the window and glance around wildly for a quick escape route. But my feet slip on a patch of ice, and I tumble onto the sidewalk. My shopping bags fly through the air and land in a messy heap.

Somehow Dane is already by my side. He extends a hand, which I grab, and he helps me up.

"Are you all right?" he asks breathlessly.

"I'm fine!"

I realize that he is still holding my hand, and I pull it away. Blushing, he reaches down and picks up my shopping bags.

"How are you?" he asks, handing the bags to me.

Embarrassed. "Good. Shopping. How are you?" I ask, brushing snow and ice from my parka.

"Fine. Actually, I'm taking the red-eye to London tonight."

"To see your family?"

"Yes."

"And, um . . . you're coming back after that?"

"Actually, I'm moving to New York City."

"You're . . . what?"

"There's really no reason for me to . . . If I'm accepted to one of the master's programs there, I'll stay on. If not, I'll relocate again next fall, to Boston or elsewhere."

"Oh!"

This news stirs up a wisp of emotion in me—sorrow, regret, *something*—and just as quickly, the wisp is gone. "Well, I hope you're happy there," I rush on. "You know, in New York City or Boston or wherever."

"Thank you."

He gives a little cough and busies himself with his gloves. I can tell he's trying not to look at me, but he is, just as I'm trying not to look at him. Why hasn't he miraculously turned old and ugly? He's still so gorgeous—even more gorgeous than before, if that's possible.

Of course, it's only been a month, and I'm being ridiculous. I shift my shopping bags from my right arm to my left and check out the fake Santa with great interest.

"So have you heard from Juilliard?" Dane is asking me.

"I'm sorry, what?"

"Are they going to give you a live audition? What about your other schools?"

"I haven't heard from anybody yet. January, I think."

"Yes, of course. I knew that. Have you picked out a piece for the twentieth-century requirement yet? For the live auditions?"

"I'm trying to decide between my Prokofiev sonata and 'Jeux d'eau.'"

"I would go with the Prokofiev. Not many people can play that, and it will impress the judges."

"Really? Okay, thanks."

"Not that you need to try hard to impress them. I'm sure you'll bowl them over, no matter what you play." Dane pauses and peers at his watch. "So, um, I'd better get home and pack."

"Of course!"

"I'm very glad we ran into each other."

I guess he's too much of a gentleman to point out that we didn't exactly run into each other. "Me too."

"I hope you have a nice Christmas."

"You too. Um, Dane?"

"Yes?"

I meet his gaze. His face is a polite mask, but his eyes, his ocean eyes, fill suddenly with hope. There is so much I want to say to him. The words, the emotions, swirl around in my head and clash against one another. Is there a future, any future, that is possible between us? I don't know. Perhaps I'll never know.

"Nothing," I murmur, turning away. "Have a safe trip."

Just then he reaches out and touches my cheek as lightly and fleetingly as a snowflake. "Will I ever see you again?" he asks softly.

I want so much to lean into his touch, but it's gone.

"Beatrice?"

"Yes. No. Maybe."

This time I walk away for real, and he doesn't try to stop me.

EPILOGUE

When Dad and I drive up to Juilliard, there is a small group of students waiting for us. Incredibly, they all start clapping and cheering, as though I were a rock star instead of a newbie nobody arriving for freshman orientation.

"What on earth?" Dad exclaims, slamming on the brakes.

One of the students gestures for Dad to pull up to the curb. We get out of the car, and the clapping and cheering continue.

"Welcome to Juilliard!"

"Don't touch those bags, we'll carry them up for you."

"You're Bea Kim, right? I remember you from audition week."

"It says here you're on the eighteenth floor."

"You have one of the A rooms, those are the biggest!"

And just like that, the five smiling students in their

matching orientation T-shirts load my luggage into a giant wheeled cart. Three of them head for a freight elevator with the cart. Two others direct us to the check-in area.

"I don't remember this kind of red-carpet treatment at MIT or Columbia," Dad says to me as we start down the sidewalk.

"Yeah, it's pretty awesome. I could get used to it."

When we reach the front entrance, Dad pauses and looks around. His eyes tear up.

"Dad?"

"Yup."

"Are you okay?"

"Yeah, I'm fine, honey. Let's go inside and get you settled."

He turns away and pinches the bridge of his nose. Oh, God, he's going to start crying. Fortunately, he won't be the only one. Just inside the revolving door, some mom is sobbing into a handkerchief.

Still, he's doing pretty well, considering.

Upstairs in the check-in area, we join the line for last names beginning with the letters *K* through *R*. A volunteer offers Dad and me bottled waters. "Are you music, dance, or drama?" she asks me cheerfully.

"Music. I'm a piano performance major."

"Hey, me too!" She points to her name tag: NAOMI, PIANO,

TORONTO, CANADA. "Welcome to Juilliard! Whose studio are you in?"

"Annaliese van Allstyne."

"Holy crap, you're *that* girl. Everyone's talking about you."

"What? Why?"

"The Schumann Fantasy and Prokofiev Six, right? A couple of the doctoral students heard your audition back in March and Totally. Freaked. Out."

I grin, embarrassed. "Really?"

"I am so going to suck up to you and become your best friend. Oh, and I can tell you how to score the best practice rooms. There's no formal sign-up system, so it's a bit nutty. The diehards will *literally* camp out with their favorite pianos so they can claim them twenty-four/seven. Other pianos, though, the action is so stiff that you can't even press the keys."

"That's good to know. Thanks!"

Naomi takes off to help out another student. Why did I think Juilliard was such a scary place? Everyone here is so nice.

After Dad and I complete the check-in process, we split up so he can deal with some forms at the registrar's office. We agree to meet on the eighteenth floor of the dormitory building in an hour, unpack my stuff, and say hi to my roommate, Sulema, who is a singer from Austin, Texas. Dad and I are planning to have dinner with Sulema and her parents later at a restaurant in the neighborhood.

But first, I decide to make a detour to the fifth floor of the main building to see if Annaliese is there. Along the way I snap some pictures—of random students, Paul Hall, the cool electronic boards that display events—and text them to Plum.

After a moment she replies:

> SO AWESOME! I'm at the mall with Mommy and Daddy buying sheets and towels!

I write:

> Get crimson ones!

We exchange lots of x's and o's and promise to talk later. I am so happy Plum got into the school of her dreams, the one with the big pink heart around it in her Golden Notebook. Over the summer she pored over the Harvard course offerings, took the online placement exams, and Skyped with her roommate, Vimbai from Zimbabwe. We've already picked out a couple of fall weekends to visit each other.

Another text comes in:

Good luck, Bumblebee.

My chest tightens. Theo. I haven't heard from him in months—not since Dad made him come to my high school graduation.

I write:

Thank you! I hope you'll visit me in NYC!

No reply.

I slip my phone into my pocket. At least he reached out. It's a start, anyway.

I make my way up to Annaliese's studio. Through the closed door, I can hear the faint strains of Debussy's "The Girl with the Flaxen Hair."

When the last chord fades away, I knock on the door.

"Yes?"

I poke my head inside. Annaliese's face lights up when she sees me. "Beatrice! You have arrived! Come in, come in."

She rises from her chair and clasps me in a warm hug. "How was your journey? Is your father here with you?"

"He's at the registrar's office."

"Perhaps we could all have lunch tomorrow? I would very much like to meet him. How are you doing? Did you work on the Schubert sonata over the summer?"

"Yes! I need your help on the second movement, though. It's so . . . " I hesitate.

"Ethereal? Understated? Yes, I know. Why don't you sit down and play a little bit of it for me?"

"Right now?"

"Please. My next appointment is not until two. Oh, and before I forget, I have something for you from Gabriel. He came by to see me before he left for Boston."

She picks up a package and hands it to me. For a second I forget to breathe. I haven't seen or spoken to Dane since last winter, when he moved to New York City. He wrote to me a few times, but I couldn't bring myself to write back. It was too hard, too confusing. And then he wrote to me in May, letting me know that he had been accepted to the Juilliard, Manhattan School of Music, and New England Conservatory master's programs and that he had chosen NEC. He didn't say why.

The package is wrapped in cream-colored paper. I unwrap it carefully. Inside is the Schumann Fantasy sheet music, although the cover looks different. Puzzled, I flip through the pages.

It is the version with the original ending, the one that contains a secret message for Clara. Clara Wieck, who later became Clara Schumann.

I scan the pages again. There is no inscription.

Annaliese peers over the top of her glasses. "What did he give you?"

"The Schumann Fantasy. The *urtext* edition, the one with the original ending."

"Ah!"

Dazed, I sit down at the Steinway and open the piece to the last movement. I put my hands on the keyboard and re-create the familiar notes. And for a moment I am transported back to that time when Dane and I were in this room together. I was a different girl, frozen in place between the past and the future. Then he held me in his arms, the first of many firsts, and my future began.

Now the music shifts and becomes unfamiliar: the other ending.

I stop. Some things are too personal, too private.

"Beatrice?"

Annaliese leans forward with a smile. "Are you ready to play the Schubert for me?"

"I'm ready."

I put aside the Schumann and reset my hands on the keyboard.

Will I ever see you again?

Yes. No. Maybe.

I close my eyes, find my breath, and begin again.

ACKNOWLEDGMENTS

First up, I want to thank Liesa Abrams, Sarah McCabe, and Annette Pollert for making me a better writer and for encouraging me to take big, scary risks. I am so lucky to have had three such capable and caring editors on this book.

I can't say enough about the rest of the Simon Pulse team, especially Mara Anastas, Mary Marotta, Kayley Hoffman, Katherine Devendorf, Sara Berko, Teresa Ronquillo, Carolyn Swerdloff, Christina Pecorale, Jodie Hockensmith, Faye Bi, and last but not least, Karina Granda, who designed the amazing cover.

I am very grateful to Lydia Wills and Nora Spiegel for finding the perfect home for *Consent* and for always believing in me.

Thank you, Cindy Nixon, for being an ace copyeditor and for loving this book.

Three experts shared their vast experience and wisdom with me in three different areas. Jens David Ohlin advised me on matters of law. Dr. Marice Pappo helped me understand my characters' messy, complicated psyches. And I owe a special debt of gratitude to Christopher Reynolds, who vetted the manuscript many times over from a pianist's perspective.

Nancy Holzner and Jeanne Mackin: I could not have written *Consent* without our caffeine-fueled mornings at The Shop. Thank you for keeping me company in the trenches, for your endless support, and for your friendship.

Hugs, chocolates, and wine to the Binders! I'm honored to be part of this smart, savvy, generous group of women.

Many thanks to my fabulous fellow bloggers at Young Adult Outside the Lines.

Huge props to the folks at We Need Diverse Books.

To all the writers, readers, bloggers, teachers, librarians, booksellers, and other book people out there: Whenever our paths cross, whether at a literary event, on the street, online, or elsewhere, I am reminded that I belong to one of the best, most interesting, most dedicated communities in the world. Let's keep it going forever.

Christa Desir, there are not enough adjectives in the dictionary to describe how awesome you are.

To my family: You are my reason for all of this. I love you guys.